# Cars, Computers, and Chaos

**Misadventure and Mystery, Volume 1**

Travis Cramer

Published by Travis Cramer, 2024.

CARS, COMPUTERS, AND CHAOS

**First edition. April 28, 2024.**

Copyright © 2024 Travis Cramer.

ISBN: 979-8227838766

Written by Travis Cramer.

# Table of Contents

Dedicated to my sister, Violet, for always, well, mostly, being happy to read my stories and give me reviews on them before anyone else!

# Cars, Computers, and Chaos

THE FIRST BOOK IN THE MISADVENTURE AND MYSTERY SERIES

By Travis Cramer

Edited by Violet Cramer

# Chapter I

S cott was hurrying home with his backpack swinging on his shoulders. It was 3 PM in the

afternoon, and he just gotten out from school. He wanted to get home as fast as he could, since he had planned to work on his robot after school. His mom would want him to mow the lawn and most likely weed out the garden as well, so he knew that he wouldn't get much time.

Scott was a tall 15-year-old boy. He had dark black hair and brown eyes. Despite his rather bearish height of 6 feet, he didn't care much for sports. He spent his free time playing guitar and messing around with computers instead. He was a computer whiz and spent a lot of his time learning how to code. His mother wanted him to join a sports team in school, but he swore that the closest he would come to sports was P.E.

As he exited the school parking lot, Scott heard someone call his name.

"Scott! Wait up."

It was Erica, one of Scott's best friends. She was carrying a textbook in her hands and chasing after Scott. Scott stopped walking and turned around.

"You left this in the cafeteria," she said, catching up to Scott and handing him the textbook. It was his biology textbook.

"Oh, thanks. I was distracted. Do you think it would make more sense for a robot to have a claw hand or a drill hand?" Scott asked, taking the book.

Erica looked at him. She was a pretty 15-year-old girl with light brown hair and blue eyes. Unlike Scott, she enjoyed sports far more than computers and music. She was the captain of the girls' soccer team and she knew the rules of practically every sport. However, like Scott, she played an instrument. Her parents had given her drum lessons when she was six, and she had really liked the instrument. Since then, she had continued to practice the drums alongside soccer and volleyball. She was smart, but she focused far more on sports than she did on academics.

"I have no idea," she said. "Ask Adrian. He knows way more about that stuff than I do."

Adrian was a friend of Scott's and Erica's. He was 16 years old and absolutely fascinated with plants. He owned one of the largest gardens in the neighborhood and was an expert when it came to naming plants. He was also great at history and knew everything about wars, dates, biographies, etc. Neither Scott nor Erica knew how he managed to learn so much about everything. They were sometimes convinced that he had found a way to make his days longer than 24 hours, since he somehow had time to learn all this and still spend time with Erica and Scott.

"Yeah, you're right." Scott nodded. "I haven't seen Adrian yet, have you?"

"I saw him leave the cafeteria, but after that, he disappeared. Probably in the library, burying his head in a book," Erica said, looking behind her. "Whoops, never mind. Here he comes now."

A boy came rushing out of the school holding his backpack by the handle.

"Hey Adrian. Where wer-?" Erica started to ask.

"Sorry, no time to talk," Adrian said, rushing by. "I've got to get home to water my Cucurbitas. Plus, my mom wants me to watch Katie."

Katie was Adrian's younger sister. She was six, and Adrian often complained about how annoying she was. Mainly he was just annoyed that he had to watch her when his parents left to go somewhere.

"Wait, what abo-"

"No time!" Adrian called over his shoulder as he dashed by.

Erica shook her head. "Makes me wonder how we met him in the first place," she said.

Scott laughed. "What the heck are Cucurbitas?" he asked. "And why on earth is he growing them?"

"Cucurbitas, also known as Cucurbits, are a plant family that includes various species of gourds, melons, squashes, and pumpkins. They have been cultivated for thousands of years for food, medicine, and other uses. It makes perfect sense for someone to grow them," said a voice from behind them.

A short red-haired girl stepped next to them.

"Oh, hi Phoebe," said Scott. "I thought you'd be in the library studying for the PSAT."

Phoebe was 14 years old and practically obsessed with colleges. She had short red hair and wore glasses, which covered her brown eyes. She was constantly studying and researching scholarships and colleges, despite only being a sophomore in high school. She always had her nose in a book and was a math and science genius. She was also an only child, with gave her time to study.

"Well, normally I would have been, but with the science fair coming up, I've been focusing on my project."

"What is your project?" asked Erica.

"I'm conducting a comparative analysis of the filtration efficacy of various water purifiers in eliminating contaminants." said Phoebe. "It's not exactly top-quality, but since I have so much other stuff going on, it was the best I could do."

"Huh?" Scott asked, puzzled. Phoebe had only recently taken up a habit of replacing all the simple words she said with more advanced and longer words. She claimed it made her sound much smarter, but it made talking to her difficult sometimes.

"I said, I have a lot of other stuff going on, so I didn't have that much time to work on my project," answered Phoebe. "I thought I made that pretty clear."

"No-I-whatever. Good luck on your science project."

"Luck? No, from a statistical standpoint, luck is a mere manifestation of the probability theory, and therefore, any attribution of its impact to external factors is essentially baseless. My project is based on skill alone. Now, if you'll excuse me, I have work to do." Phoebe said, hurrying off.

Scott looked at Erica. "I really wish Phoebe would stop talking like that," he complained. "Does she not realize that it doesn't matter how smart she sounds, if nobody understands her?"

Erica shrugged, pulling a basketball out of her bag. "Do you want to come to the park and shoot some hoops with me? Last time I played with Teddy he started crying, and Mom got mad at me."

Teddy was Erica's younger brother. He was eight and he also liked sports. Erica practiced with him a lot, but he always got upset that she was so much better than him, so she was looking for a new partner. She had tried practicing with her younger sister, Lucy, who was Teddy's twin, but Lucy had never cared much about sports.

Scott shook his head. "Sorry, I've got to get home. Mom has probably got a list of chores for me to do and I want to build my robot. Maybe tomorrow."

"Nope. Tomorrow I've got to be at swimming practice right after school." Erica had swimming practice every Tuesday and Thursday. It was just another one of the many sports that she played.

"How about Wednesday?" Scott tried.

"No can do. I have softball at 4."

"What days are you not busy?" Scott asked.

Erica pulled out her phone. The screen and back of the phone were cracked and the camera was covered in scratches. Years of playing sports had taken a toll on the phone. She opened her calendar and scanned it.

"Today's my only free day," she said.

"Seriously? You have something *every* day of the week except for Monday?" Scott asked in disbelief.

"Well, normally I would have skating today, but the rink is closed for repairs, so I'm free this evening. Say, did you hear about Old Man McGinnis?"

"You mean the old guy that lives on Greenlowe Road? No, what happened to him?" Scott asked, curious.

"I heard that his car got stolen. He left it parked right in front of his house and when he went out in the morning, it was gone."

"Man, that's terrible. I feel bad for him; he's such a nice guy. How did you hear about that?"

"His granddaughter plays defense on the soccer team. She was telling everyone about it."

"Wow, well I hope the police find it soon. He doesn't deserve to have his car stolen. I gotta run, though. I'll see you tomorrow."

"Yeah, see you tomorrow," Erica said distractedly. Then she turned and started walking towards the basketball courts.

Scott checked his watch. It was a quarter past 3. "Shoot," he said to no one in particular. "I've gotta get home."

He broke into a run and headed down the road. He saw Phoebe walking down the road wearing headphones and looking at her phone. There was no sidewalk where she was walking, and Phoebe hated walking in grass. Suddenly, a speeding car came bearing down the road and right towards Phoebe!

"Phoebe, look out!" yelled Scott. She didn't move. Scott dashed towards Phoebe and tackled her into the grass next to the road as the car sped by.

"Oof!" Phoebe said as Scott landed on her. "What was that for?"

"Did you seriously not just see that car drive by?" Scott asked, incredulously. "It nearly killed you."

Phoebe shook her head. "According to my calculations, the probability of being struck by an automobile whilst traversing this leisurely thoroughfare is exceedingly low."

Scott blinked. "Speak English!" he said.

Phoebe rolled her eyes and said "The odds of getting hit by a car on this road are slim."

Scott raised his hands in defeat. "Why couldn't you have just said that?"

"Utilizing such a mode of speech indicates a relatively diminished level of intellectual capacity."

Scott stood up. "Don't even bother," he muttered. "Just be careful when you walk."

Phoebe brushed the grass and leaves off her skirt. "I shall endeavor to exercise due caution whilst promenading upon the thoroughfare, all for the sake of providing you with a sense of ease and tranquility."

Scott shook his head and rolled his eyes at the same time. He waved goodbye to Phoebe and headed home. His older brother, Gregory, greeted him with a "Hey" when he knocked on the door. Gregory was 18 and often watched Scott while their parents worked.

Scott's parents owned a small mom and pop shop a few miles away from their house. They couldn't afford to hire that many employees, so they had to do a lot of the stuff themselves, which meant that Scott would often be left with Gregory, or Greg as most people called him.

"You're late," Greg commented, looking at the clock. "Were you playing basketball or something?"

"No, I-uh got sidetracked by a speeding car." Scott told Greg about what happened to Phoebe.

Greg whistled. "Dang. Mom and Dad would probably take my car away from me if I drove like that."

Greg had gotten his license a year ago and he had saved up his money to buy a cheap SUV. It was a Jeep, and he was very proud of it. Sometimes, if he was in a good mood, he would take Scott to go somewhere in his car.

Scott nodded. "Yeah. Did you hear the Old Man McGinnis' car got stolen? Erica told me about it," he said.

Greg pointed to the window. "That must why I've been seeing cop cars drive up and down this road all the time."

"Most likely. I-"

Scott was interrupted by his cell phone ringing. "Hang on a minute," he said to Greg.

He looked at his cell phone. It was Adrian calling.

"Hey, Adrian. What's up?" Scott asked.

"Scott! Someone ran over my flower garden!" Adrian sounded like he was almost in tears. "It's completely ruined."

"Whoa, whoa, back up a bit," said Scott. "What do you mean, someone 'ran over them'? Isn't your garden in the back of your house?"

"My vegetable garden is, but my flower garden needs more early morning sunlight, so I had to plant it closer to the road. My flowers were still at least 5 feet away from the road, though."

"How do you know someone ran over them?"

"I saw the tire tracks! They are too flat to have been caused by someone stepping on them. Just come over, please." Adrian sounded flustered.

"Okay, I'll be right over," Scott said, hanging up the phone.

"Who was that?" asked Greg, after Scott had hung up.

"It was Adrian," Scott answered. "Apparently someone ran over his plants. He wants me to come over."

"You still have homework, don't you?" Greg asked.

"Yes, but I'll be right back. I-shoot!" Scott paused mid-sentence. "My bike is still broken. I never got around to repairing it. Can you drive me?"

Scott had broken his bike a week prior after biking over a fallen tree branch and bending the handlebars.

Greg raised an eyebrow. "I'm pretty sure that Adrian's house is in walking distance."

"Yes, I know it is, but I really don't feel like walking half a mile. C'mon, please. It'll be quick."

Greg rolled his eyes. "Fine, but only because I have to go pick up some food for Winston."

Winston was Greg's pet fish. He had been trying to teach it tricks, but it never seemed to want to do anything except swim around.

"Thanks! You're the best," Scott told Greg.

"Yeah, whatever. Let's just go," Greg said, grabbing his keys.

Greg and Scott got into the car and Scott climbed into the front seat.

"Uh-uh. Back seat," Greg said, pointing behind him. "Last time you sat in the front seat, you wouldn't stop changing the radio station."

Scott shrugged and climbed into the back seat. Greg started the car and pulled out of the driveway. They were at Adrian's house in less than 5 minutes.

"Okay, I'll pick you up in about 15 minutes, okay?" Greg said.

Scott nodded and knocked on Adrian's door. The door opened a crack and a little girl's head poked out.

"What do you want?" she asked.

"Hi, Katie. Is Adrian there?" Scott asked.

"Yep. He's in his room. I wouldn't go in there, though," Katie answered.

"Why's that?" asked Scott.

"He's pretty upset," Katie replied, pulling the door open. Adrian's head appeared at the top of the stairwell.

"Hi, Scott," Adrian said.

"Hey, Adrian. Why exactly did you want me to come over?" Scott said.

Adrian walked down the stairs. "Here, follow me." To Katie he said, "Stay inside."

"Wait, but I'm hungry," Katie complained.

Adrian sighed. "Go eat an apple and peanut butter or something. Mom and Dad just went shopping. There's plenty to eat."

"Okay!" said Katie, skipping off.

Adrian shook his head and opened the door. He pointed towards the corner of the road at the end of his property.

"Look over there," he said, pointing to a large patch of wilted flowers.

Scott walked over to them and looked closely. They had definitely been run over. There was no question about it. What was once a beautiful and colorful garden of flowers was reduced to a clump of wilted leaves and smashed stems. There was no repairing it.

"Oof," he said. "I'm sorry about this. Do you know who did it?"

Adrian shook his head again. "My parents never put up security cameras. We live in a fairly safe neighborhood. This is probably the worst thing to ever happen."

Scott knelt down and looked at the flowers. "I'm pretty sure that this qualifies as an actual crime. Maybe not the running over the flowers, but this is at least trespassing."

Adrian nodded. "Sure, but what will the police do? Most people don't understand the importance of flower gardens. The police will just tell me to suck it up."

"You're right. The police typically don't care about crimes like this." He looked at the tire tracks. "I wonder..."

"You wonder what?" Erica pulled up behind Scott on her bike. It was a mountain bike with 30" off-road tires and a light aluminum frame. Erica's parents had got it for her 13th birthday.

Scott jumped, startled. He turned around to see Erica. "I'll never understand why that bike is so quiet. A giant bike like that should be pretty loud," he said, annoyed.

Erica smirked. "I got your text. Sorry about what happened," she said, turning to Adrian.

"Thanks," Adrian replied. "I can't believe it. 2 years of work, ruined by one bad driver." He turned away. "I'll have to start all over again."

"Hey, whoa. It might not be that bad," Erica said. "We'd all be happy to help you plant them again. Right, Scott?"

Erica elbowed Scott in the side.

"Ouch, wha- Of course we'll help you plant more flowers," said Scott.

Adrian smiled. "Thanks guys. But it's not that simple. I'll have to dig out all these flowers, buy more seeds, and then wait for months after I've planted them, before my garden even starts to look remotely the same." He frowned. "Seeds aren't cheap. At least the good ones aren't. I used to get my seeds at the dollar store, but they never worked very well. You have to get them from nurseries, and they can cost as much as $20 a packet."

Erica whistled. "That's a lot of money. How can you afford that?"

"That's the problem! I can't afford it! I worked for my neighbor almost every day after school to earn enough money to buy the seeds, and now it's all gone. I don't have the money to buy the seeds, since I had to keep buying fertilizer."

"How much money did you spend?" Scott broke in.

Adrian shrugged. "Over a thousand dollars, at least," he said. "But that's counting all the plants, fertilizer, pots, and everything. I don't know how much of that was spent on flowers. Probably a couple hundred."

Erica shook her head. "That's too much money to lose. The police have to do something about it. You should tell them."

"I'll tell them, but it won't do any good," said Adrian, with a doubtful look.

"Adrian is correct," said a voice from behind them. It sounded like Phoebe's.

Erica and Scott whirled around. There was no one there.

Scott scratched his head. "Am I going crazy?" he asked. He looked at Erica. "Did you hear that too."

Eric nodded. "I did!"

# Chapter II

"Me too," echoed Adrian. "What the heck is- oh." He pointed upwards. Erica squinted and looked towards the sky. There was a small drone hovering above them, its wings buzzing quietly.

"Phoebe?" asked Scott.

"Your assumptions are correct," said the drone in Phoebe's voice.

"What the heck is that thing?" asked Adrian. "And why are you using it to spy on us?"

The drone landed at Scott's feet. "This is a drone, quite obviously. And I am not spying on you. I wish to clarify that I am merely using it to listen to you three."

"Yeah. I don't know about you, but that's the definition of spying," said Scott, sarcastically.

"I received Adrian's text about the damage done to his garden. I first wish to give my condolences, and second to give some advice," the drone said.

"How can you hear what we are saying? How is your voice coming out of that drone?" Erica asked.

"That is unrelated to the topic at hand, but I will relieve you of the burden on your brain by enlightening you on the design of this drone. There is a microphone connected to the remote control for the drone. It picks up my voice and relays it back to the drone, which then plays the voice out of a speaker. As for hearing you three, it is the same principle, except the microphone is on the drone and the speaker in the controller. The drone is also equipped with a camcorder, which enables me to see you as well as hear you."

"Well, that's great and all, but why couldn't you have just come here in person instead of sending your pet here?" Scott asked.

"Since my science project requires my utmost attention, I could not spare the time needed to bike to Adrian's house. I instead did the next best thing and sent a drone over," Phoebe answered. "Now may I present to you my suggestion?"

"Yes, of course," Adrian broke in.

"Very well. As I stated before, Adrian is correct in saying that the police will not help in locating the perpetrator who committed this heinous crime. Therefore, I suggest that we bring back the group known as SEAP."

There was silence for a while. Then Erica spoke. "You think that we should bring back a goofy club that we had when we were in grade school?"

"Precisely," Phoebe said.

SEAP was a detective club that the four of them had created year ago. They mostly solved simple "crimes" such as missing items and other frivolous things. They had eventually all gotten too busy to keep the club going, and it just stopped. The name had come from merging the first letters of all their names into one word. Phoebe had complained about this, saying that it should be PEAS, not SEAP, but Erica had said that nobody would take them seriously if they named their club PEAS.

"What good will that do?" Scott asked. "All we did was find people's missing shoes and pencils. Half the time they just misplaced them. It was just a silly little club that we did to earn a quarter now and then."

Scott had proposed charging a quarter if they solved the case. It was a pretty good idea, and they had made at least $20 from finding missing items.

The drone flew in front of Scott and at his eye level.

"I agree, but now that we have grown in age and hopefully in maturity, I believe that we have the potential to solve more difficult and advanced crimes," Phoebe said.

Erica snorted. "As if any of us have the ability to solve crimes. I can barely find my toothbrush in the morning. I suggest that we leave this up to the police."

"Once again, the entities known as the 'police' will not endeavor to help us in capturing the perpetrator of such a minuscule crime," Phoebe said in a nasally voice. "I had thought that you three would be far more receptive to the idea of re-creating our detective agency."

"Phoebe, we are teenagers. It just isn't realistic," said Adrian. "None of us can drive, which means that we have no way of getting anywhere on our own, short of biking or walking. And that's just one of the problems. There's a whole load more."

The drone flew away with a whizzing sound. Scott watched it. "I think that we might have made her mad," he said.

"I mean, she was right about one thing," said Adrian. "The police aren't going to do anything about this. But we can't either."

"Why not?" asked Scott suddenly. "Why can't we do anything about this?"

"Well, because we have no way of locating the person, and even if we do, we can't get there. And even if we could, what are we supposed to do then? Arrest them? We're teenagers, not professional detectives," Erica said, tossing her hair back.

"It's not like we would be trying to catch a murderer here. We're just trying to catch a bad driver and make him pay Adrian back for the damage that he did to his flower bed," Scott said. "Come on, Phoebe was right. It's at least worth a shot."

Erica sighed. "You too now? What is up with that 'detective' agency? Why do you guys want to bring it back now?"

"We don't even have to make a detective agency. Why don't we just help out Adrian and find the driver? Honestly, how hard can it be?"

Erica shook her head. "I think this is a waste of time," she said. "But if you're determined, I'll help you and Phoebe."

"I'll help too," Adrian chimed in. "After all, they are my plants, and I'm the one who's losing if we don't catch the driver."

"Good enough," said Scott. He saw Greg's car approaching down the road. "I've gotta run, but I'll send a text in the group chat about this."

He waved goodbye and hopped into Greg's car. There was an oversize box in the trunk, which peaked Scott's curiosity.

"Greg, what's in the box?" he asked.

"Don't get your hopes up," Greg replied from the front seat. "It's just a new lawn mower. Dad told me to go pick it up while they were at the store. I was supposed to pick it up before you got home, but I, errrr, forgot."

"Well, I guess it was time we got a new lawn mower," said Scott. "Our old one keeps getting jammed every time it goes over something thick."

"Yep," replied Greg, pulling into the driveway. "I'll get the mower out later. Go do your homework."

Scott rolled his eyes. He walked inside and grabbed his bag, setting it on top of his desk. He pulled out his laptop and opened his essay that his English teacher, Mrs. Johnson, had assigned.

"A Comparison Between the Causes for WWI and WWII"

It was a boring essay, to be sure, but Scott liked history. He was glad that his English professor had assigned them a history topic rather than a boring science or worse still, a social studies topic. Of course, all those paled in comparison to awful introspective essays. Scott hated them. He was never comfortable giving those essays back to Mrs. Johnson and he always blanked out when trying to think of things to write.

Scott was musing over the topic when his phone vibrated. It was a text from Erica in the group chat. It read:

"When do u guys want to meet? And where?"

Scott typed back: "Wait 'till afternoon. Have homework to do."

Phoebe sent a message: "The sooner, the better. I have pictures of the tire tracks."

She sent a bunch of photos of Adrian's garden, plus a few pictures that were zoomed into the tire tracks.

Erica typed, "How do we figure out what car those tracks belong to?"

This was Scott's territory. His dad was a huge car nut, and he owned volumes and volumes of encyclopedias filled with car information.

"My dad has a book of car tires and the tracks they make," Scott typed. "I'll browse through that book l8er."

Adrian joined the chat, "Mom wants me to watch Katie in the evening. I can't leave the house," he sent.

"Y don't we just meet in your house?" Erica asked.

Scott liked that idea. It made sense, considering that they were trying to figure out what happened to Adrian's plants. He sent a thumbs-up emoji.

"That is a feasible option," Phoebe sent.

"That works, but only if we don't mind Katie listening to us," Adrian replied.

"Should be fine. We aren't talking about anything super-secret." Erica sent.

"Then are we all in agreement?" Phoebe asked.

Scott, Erica, and Adrian all sent thumbs-up emojis.

"Okay, we meet at Adrian's house at 5pm to discuss details about the case. Clear your schedule." Phoebe sent.

Scott was about to send a message to Phoebe, telling her not to call it a "case", but he decided he didn't want to get in an argument with Phoebe and went back to writing his report.

Greg poked his head into Scott's room. "Hey, Mom and Dad texted me. They said that they are going to be late. There was an accident at the store," he said.

Scott turned around pulled out his earbuds. "What?" he asked.

Greg bunched his eyebrows. "I said that Mom and Dad are going to be late coming home today. "

"Oh, okay. I'm going over to Adrian's house at 5, anyway," Scott answered, pausing his music.

"You are? Didn't you just go there?" Greg asked.

"I did, but Adrian wanted me, Phoebe, and Erica to help him figure out who wrecked his garden. I said that we could go over there after I finished with my homework."

"Okay, whatever. I'm not driving you, though. I've got a job interview at 5:30."

"Wait, you do? Where are you going?" Greg was starting college in a few months, but he was looking for a summer job so he didn't spend the entire summer bumming around.

"Nowhere, I'm staying home. The interview is online. Do not interrupt me unless the house is burning down, do you understand?" Greg couldn't stand it when Scott interrupted him in the middle of something, no matter how un-important whatever he was doing.

"Geez, fine. I'll be at Adrian's anyway, so you get the house to yourself. Now go away so I can finish this stupid report." Scott said, turning back to his desk.

Greg shut the door and walked out. Right after he left, Scott's phone started to ring. It was a group call between all of them, started by Erica.

Scott picked up. "Hi, what's going on?" he asked.

"You guys are not going to believe this," said Erica. "My sister's car just got stolen."

Erica had an older sister who was 30. She was moved out and Erica rarely ever saw her, since by the time Erica was 3, her sister was already heading off to college."

"Sister? Lucy doesn't have a car, last time I checked," Adrian said, sounding puzzled.

"No, not Lucy! Penelope's car." Erica said, sounding agitated.

"Penelope?" asked Adrian. "You have a sister named Penelope?"

"Yes, I do. She's 15 years older than me, and we rarely ever talk, but yes, I have an older sister." Erica said.

"Lucky," muttered Scott. "All I have is an older brother."

"I barely knew her, okay. But that's not the point. The point is that there's been two different car thefts in the same town in the same week." Erica exclaimed.

"That's peculiar. Was your sister in possession of a highly coveted car?" Phoebe asked.

"No idea," said Erica. "I'm not really a car person. She had a sedan, I think."

"Unhelpful," stated Phoebe. "There are millions of different sedan makes and models. I am going to need a much more descriptive statement."

"I don't know, okay!" Erica said. "I really don't care what car people drive, as long as it runs."

"Well, my utmost apologies to your sister for the loss of her car, but I'm not sure what we can do about this. We are not private investigators, nor are we police officers," said Phoebe.

"There's nothing to do about it, okay! I just thought you guys might be interested in knowing that. Gosh!" Erica said, annoyed.

"I wonder if this could be related to Old Man McGinnis' car. You think it's the same person," asked Scott.

"Hmm, good point," said Erica. "But why would someone come to this town and start stealing cars?"

Scott furrowed his eyebrows. "Good question," he said. "It's not like this is a high-end town or anything."

"Let's discuss this later when we come to my house," said Adrian. "I've gotta run. Katie is freaking out because we ran out of bananas."

"Yeah, thanks for letting us know," said Scott to Erica. "I've still got homework to do, so I'll see you guys later." He left the call and turned back to his laptop. He stared at the screen, trying to think of what to write. Eventually, he quit and started on his math homework.

# Chapter III

The hour and a half passed slowly for Scott, but eventually he finished his homework and grabbed a snack from the kitchen. It was 4:45pm and Greg was busy preparing for his interview. Scott knocked on Greg's door.

Greg pulled the door open, wearing sweatpants, a button-down shirt and two different pairs of shoes.

"What do you want?" he demanded.

Scott tried to hide a laugh, but he couldn't. He burst out laughing, much to the annoyance of Greg.

"I'm trying to figure out what to wear for my interview," he said. "Now what do you want."

"I'm-going-over-to-Adrian's-house," Scott answered, in between laughs. "I'll be back in about an hour. Shoot me a text if Mom and Dad come home."

"Fine, whatever." Greg pulled off a shoe and tossed it across his room. "Just leave me alone."

Scott grinned and walked away. Then he sighed, realizing that he still hadn't fixed his bike and he would have to walk to Adrian's house. He walked out the door and looked at his bike. He tried to ride it, but it was just too hard to ride with the bent handlebar.

He shook his head and started walking over to Adrian's house. It took him about 20 minutes, but eventually he made it. Erica and Phoebe were already there and they were all standing around Adrian's garden.

"There you are," said Erica. "What took you so long?"

"Sorry, my bike is broken," Scott answered. "I had to walk here."

Scott walked over to the plants. Not much had changed from the last time they were there, which wasn't really surprising, considering that they had only been gone a few hours.

"Scott, did you find anything about those tire tracks?" asked Adrian.

"Huh, what?" Scott looked up from the garden. "No, I couldn't tell from the picture. I brought the book over here, so I could get a closer look."

Scott pulled the book out of his bag. "Here," he said, opening the book. "This was the closest pattern I could find to the tracks."

Phoebe pulled the book closer. "Hmmm, the Dodge Durango 2012. This car seems familiar."

"Finally!" Scott said. "I was waiting for you to give up that stupid way of talking. You don't need to talk like an encyclopedia to sound intelligent."

"Yes, well, it was getting tiring" Phoebe said. "And even though it certainly made me sound much smarter, I decided it wasn't worth it."

Adrian laughed. "It didn't make you sound smarter. It just made nobody understand you."

Phoebe rolled her eyes. "This car," she said, pointing to the book, "Is the same make and model of the car that was stolen from Mr. McGinnis."

"It's Old Man McGinnis, Phoebe," said Erica. "Nobody calls him Mr. McGinnis. And how can you be certain about that?"

"Trust me. I have a photographic memory. This is the same type of car that Mr. McGinnis owns. Or owned, anyway," Phoebe said.

"Sooo, the person who stole *Old Man McGinnis'* car drove over Adrian's flower bed. What on earth for?" Scott asked.

"It might not have been on purpose," Adrian said. "He probably just wasn't paying attention because he was worried someone would catch him with the car and he drove off the road by mistake."

"Excellent deduction, Adrian," said Phoebe. "However, we now have a more serious problem. If-"

"Wait a minute. How can we be sure that this car happens to be McGinnis' car? I'm sure that there are multiple people who own a Dodge Dur-whatever it's called." Erica said.

There was silence for a bit.

"We may have jumped to conclusions..." said Phoebe. "I suppose there is no direct evidence to link this car to Mr. McGinnis' car, but one must admit that it seems strange that a car of the very same make and model that was stolen happened to drive into Adrian's flower garden."

"Well, that's great." said Scott. "We are now one step closer to solving the mystery. Except, not really. What good is knowing what car smashed his flowers, if we have no idea where to find that car.

"Someone must have a security camera, right?" asked Adrian. "We don't, but maybe somebody else's security camera caught the car driving away."

Scott thought for a while. It was certainly an idea, but he wasn't sure how to follow up on it.

"I'm sure people do have security cameras, but how do we get access to that footage?" he asked. "We can't just knock-on people's doors and ask to see their security camera footage."

"And why is that?" asked Phoebe.

"Because-because-it's weird," Scott sputtered. "It's not something that people do."

Phoebe raised her eyebrows. "You mean that you don't want to do it."

"No, I mean that if someone knocked on your door and asked them to see your security camera footage, would you not think that they are weird?" Scott said.

"So?" asked Erica. "So they think that we are weird. Do you want to help Adrian or not?"

"I'm inclined to agree with Scott on this," Adrian said. "It's not really polite to randomly ask people about their security camera."

"Geez, just tell them that someone ran over your flower bed," said Erica. "I'm sure that they would be happy to help you. We may as well start asking now. Do your next-door neighbors have a camera outside?"

"I-wha? I don't know!" Adrian said. "And even if they do, I'm not asking them to see their footage. We aren't cops; just a bunch of teenagers."

Phoebe sighed. "Fine. You and Scott stay here and investigate the crime scene and Erica and I will talk to people. How is that?"

"Crime scene?" asked Scott. "How is this a crime scene?"

"That is beside the point, but this could be considered vandalism, which is a crime." Phoebe said. "Now, you stay here and see what you can find."

"Okay..." Scott said hesitantly. "I'm not really sure what I'm looking for here, but we'll see what we can find."

"Good," said Phoebe. "Now Erica and I will go ask your neighbors if they have cameras facing the road. We should be back within the hour."

"Good luck," said Scott under breath as Phoebe and Erica walked away. Scott turned to Adrian.

"Well, if they don't care about embarrassing themselves, that's their problem, not mine" he said.

Adrian was looking at his ruined garden. "This garden is pretty hard to hit. Who could have been this bad of a driver?"

"I'm not sure. But Phoebe wanted us to look at it and see what we could find, so let's do that." Scott answered.

Scott knelt down in front of the garden and looked closely at the tire tracks. He was sticking his finger in the dirt when something caught his eye. It was a shiny quarter, and it looked like it hadn't been there very long.

"Hey, Adrian. Come look at this," Scott called.

Adrian walked over. "What is it?" he asked.

"This quarter," he said, pointing to the quarter lying in the dirt.

Adrian leaned over to pick it up, but Scott batted his hand away.

"Don't touch it," he said. "It could have fingerprints on it."

"Fingerprints? What are you, a private detective?" asked Adrian. "How are you going to get fingerprints off a quarter?"

"Simple," answered Scott. "Do you have a pair of gloves or a towel?"

"Sure, I always keep a pair of gardening gloves next to my garden," said Adrian.

Scott slipped on the pair of gloves that was lying next to the garden and carefully picked up the quarter.

"Let's bring this inside, and I'll teach you about Detecting 101," he said, walking towards Adrian's house. Adrian followed suit, and soon they were both sitting at the kitchen table.

"Now, let's see." Scott scratched his head. "Do you have any Baby Powder?"

"Yeah, I think I have some in the bathroom," Adrian answered. "Mom will be furious if you waste it, though."

"Don't worry," said Scott. "I won't use much of it. Just a pinch."

"All right," Adrian said, shrugging his shoulders. He left to get the baby powder and came back a minute later holding a container of it. He handed it to Scott.

Scott picked up the container and shook out a little of it onto the quarter until there was a fine coat of power over all of the quarter.

"Perfect," said Scott. "Now I need some clear tape."

"Tape. Yeah, I think I have some in my room. Hang on."

Adrian headed upstairs and came back down with a mostly empty tape roll."

"Sorry, I've been meaning to refill it," he said. "There should still be a bit left, though."

"Just need a small piece," Scott answered, pulling off a piece and handing the tape roll back to Adrian.

Scott stuck the piece of tape on the quarter and lightly pushed down. He then blew away the excess power and gently pulled the tape of the quarter. A faint, but clear fingerprint could be seen when Scott held the tape up to the light.

Scott showed the fingerprint to Adrian, but Adrian shook his head. "Dude, it's a quarter. There could be thousands of people who have touched that quarter. That one fingerprint doesn't mean anything," he said.

"No, this is the most recent one," said Scott. "All the other fingerprints have been smudged, but this one is still here. That means that it belongs to the last person who touched the quarter. Only question is: How did it get in your flower bed?"

Adrian shrugged. "For all I know, that's my quarter. I could have dropped it there last time I watered my plants. Or maybe Katie dropped it there. Or some random person walking down the street could have dropped it there. Man, it's a quarter! It could belong to anyone."

Meanwhile, Phoebe and Erica were making zero progress. They had knocked almost all the neighbor's doors near Scott's house and people either didn't have security camera, or simply weren't willing to show the footage to Phoebe and Erica.

"Well, I guess Scott was right," said Erica. "This is a waste of time. Most people aren't willing to show their security camera footage to two random teenagers."

"No," said Phoebe. "We just aren't doing this the right way."

Erica sighed. "We've already knocked on about ten different houses and I'm kind of tired of having doors slammed in my face."

Phoebe gestured to a house about 3 doors down. "Let's try that house. This time, let me do the talking."

"Whatever," Erica said, shrugging as she followed Phoebe.

Phoebe walked up to the house and knocked on the door. After they waited for about a minute, a man with a beard opened the door and asked,

"Can I help you?"

Phoebe gestured for Erica not to say anything and said "Why, yes sir. We were hoping you could spare a few minutes of your time."

"Depends. What do you need?" the man asked.

"I was wondering if you possess a contemporary security camera that happens to be oriented towards the road? And if by any chance you do, would you be inclined to grant us access to scrutinize the captured footage?" Phoebe answered.

The man squinted. "Kid, I failed high school. I have no idea what you just said," he said.

Phoebe rolled her eyes. "Allow me to repeat myself. Do you posses-"

"Do you happen to have a security camera that faces the road?" Erica interrupted.

The man raised his eyebrows. "I do," he said. "Why?"

Phoebe started to open her mouth, but Erica held up her hand.

"One of our friends had their flower garden run over. We are hoping that someone had footage of the car driving away," she said.

The man nodded his head. "Sure, I guess I can let you see the footage," he said. "Come on inside."

Phoebe and Erica stepped inside.

"My security camera is hooked up to the internet, and it automatically uploads the footage to my server," the man said. "I should be able to view the footage directly from my computer."

The man led them into a small room filled with computers, phones, and other electronics. He walked over to one of the computers and turned on the monitor.

"Sorry about the mess," he said. "This is where all my work gets done, but it rarely ever gets cleaned."

He opened up a folder on his computer marked "SECFOOT" and opened a video file. "Here we are," he said. "Around what time was your friend's flower garden run over?"

"Hmm, let me see. It was shortly after we got out of school, so after 3, but-" Erica started.

"It was at 3:27 PM," announced Phoebe. Phoebe had a photographic memory and was excellent at remembering dates and times. This often annoyed the rest of the group, but it was very useful at times, such as now.

"3:27 PM, you say," the man said, scrolling through all of his footage. "It should be right here..."

The man scrolled past 1pm, 2pm, but 3pm didn't appear.

"Hmm, that's weird," he said. "He scrolled back a bit, but there was no 3pm. The man scratched his head.

"Now that *is* strange. No reason that should be missing..." the man muttered.

Phoebe looked at Erica and they exchanged glances. "Err, is there something wrong, sir?" Erica asked.

The man turned around. "I can't seem to find the footage for the time that you said."

"Are you sure it didn't get deleted or anything?" Erica asked.

"No, it's just one long video file. There's no simple way to delete part of it. You'd have to manually edit it out, and I know that I didn't do that. It's almost like the camera just stopped videotaping and then started again."

"It could be a problem with the hardware," Phoebe said. "All electronics fail eventually, especially in crucial times." She smiled. "That's Murphy's Law. I don't believe in any of them, of course, but they are still lots of fun."

"Yeah, I guess it could be," the man answered. "I don't know why it would just stop recording like that, though. That's really strange."

"Perhaps you should get a technician to look at it," Phoebe suggested.

"Yeah, maybe. Sorry I can't help you guys though. I really don't know what's up with my camera system. Hope you catch the bad driver, though."

"It's okay," said Phoebe. "I'm sure there's someone else who has a security camera."

Phoebe and Erica left the building with less hope then with they started.

"Man, talk about bad luck. We find the only person who has a security camera and the one section of the video that we need is missing." Erica shook her head. "Not much left to do now, is there?"

Phoebe shrugged. "As much as I hate saying this, I'm very much stumped."

"I'd hate to return to Adrian without any new information, though," Erica said. "He'll be really disappointed. You're sure we've been to everyone's house?"

"Well, according to my log book-." Phoebe flipped open a notebook and skimmed through the pages. "We've hit every house except for Mr. McGinnis' house. Perhaps he has security cameras."

"Old Man McGinnis? No way," said Erica. "Didn't his car just get stolen. If he had security cameras, he'd know who stole his car."

"It is entirely possible that Mr. McGinnis does indeed have security cameras and the perpetrator of the car was simply not in view, but perhaps the person who vandalized Adrian's garden is," Phoebe answered.

"Fine, whatever." Erica rolled her eyes. "We'll go to McGinnis' house, but I'm saying 'I told you so' when he tells us he doesn't have cameras."

Back at Adrian's house, Scott was busy analyzing the fingerprint on the quarter while Adrian was sitting on the couch a few feet away.

"Dude, give it up already. It's just a fingerprint. What do you hope to find?" Adrian said, cracking open a soda.

"Well, you never know," Scott said, not taking his eyes off the quarter. "There's always a chance...Besides, don't you want to know who destroyed your flower bed?"

"I mean, I do, and thanks for all your help, but what do you hope to get out of one fingerprint?" Adrian asked. "You can't tell who it belongs to just by looking at it."

"Yeah, you're right. It's our only clue, though. Other than that, we've got nothing." Scott sighed. "Hopefully Phoebe and Erica are having more luck."

"Yeah." Adrian looked out the window at his garden. "I guess I could start over again. I've got about $300 saved up, but I was going to use it to buy a garden fence."

"No, that's ridiculous!" Scott interjected. "The person who ran over your flower bed is going to pay you back for all the seeds and plants."

"If we ever catch him," muttered Adrian.

"We are going to catch him," Scott said confidently. "And once he pays you back, we'll all help you start your garden again."

"Thanks for the offer, Scott," Adrian said, "But honestly, be realistic. We have one fingerprint, and a quarter. Neither of those things help us out at all."

"Well, we also know what kind of car the guy drives. A Dodge Durango 2012," Scott said. "Why don't we go around the neighborhood and see if we can spot that car parked on the street or maybe in someone's driveway."

Adrian stood up from the couch and chucked his soda can at the trash.

"I have to stay here and take care of Katie," he said. "You can go and scan driveways, but Mom will kill me if I leave Katie home alone." He checked his watch. "It's getting late anyway. You should probably head home."

"What about Phoebe and Erica?" Scott asked. "Shouldn't they be coming back soon? They've been gone for nearly an hour and a half."

"You're right." Adrian looked at his phone. "They didn't text us," he said. "Maybe they found something out."

Scott stared out the window. "Yeah, maybe. I hope they didn't run into any problems." He started packing up his backpack. "I'm gonna get going. I don't want to walk home in the dark. Text me when Phoebe and Erica come back." Scott slung his backpack around his back and headed home.

At the same time, Phoebe and Erica were standing on the front stoop of Old Man McGinnis' house, knocking at the door. After standing there, knocking, for about 2 minutes, Erica stepped off the stoop.

"Let's go, Phoebe," she said. "It's getting dark and I have to get back before my parents do. He's obviously not home."

Phoebe sighed. "Fine, we can try again tomorrow. I guess I should work on my science project anyway."

"Geez, Phoebe. Do you ever stop thinking about school?" Erica chuckled.

"Of course not," Phoebe said. "Without school and learning, life would be a complete waste of time."

Phoebe and Erica started walking back towards Adrian's house when they heard the door to McGinnis' house open. Erica turned around and saw a boy with a large hoodie on poking his head out the door. Erica tapped Phoebe on the shoulder and pointed towards the door.

They started walking back towards the house and Erica called out "Hi, is Mr. McGinnis home?"

The boy ignored them and went back inside the house, letting the door close behind them. Phoebe and Erica looked at each other, confused.

"What do we do now?" Erica asked Phoebe.

"Let's knock again. Someone is clearly home," Phoebe answered, walking up the front step and knocking.

This time the door opened and a woman answered. "How can I help you?" she asked.

"Hi, is Mr. McGinnis home?" asked Erica.

The woman raised an eyebrow. "Maybe. Who's asking?" she answered.

"Oh, I'm Erica and this is my friend Phoebe." We were hoping to ask Mr. McGinnis a few questions." Erica said.

The woman nodded. "Well, he is home, but now's really not a good time. He isn't feeling too great right now, so maybe come back later?"

"Oh, that's too bad," said Erica. "I hope he feels better soon. We can ask him another time; it wasn't urgent anyway."

"Thank you, I'll let Mr. McGinnis know that you stopped by. What did you say your names were again?" The woman asked.

"Oh, I'm Erica and this is Phoebe," Erica answered.

"Phoebe and Erica. Got it," the woman said, closing the door.

Erica and Phoebe stood at the door for about a minute after the woman had closed it. "So what do we do know," Erica asked. "We have still gathered absolutely no new information."

"Well, the weather report says that the sun is going down at 8:45pm tonight, and since it's already 9:15, I suggest we get back home before it gets pitch black," Phoebe said. "We can always continue our quest for information tomorrow."

"Wait a minute," Erica interjected. "Didn't you just say a few minutes ago that you didn't want to go home without any new information, and now you are suggesting that we quit?"

Phoebe shrugged. "I did say that, but I believe that our safety is more important than any information that we may, however unlikely, acquire. Hence, we should go home."

"Fine, you're right," said Erica. "Although I'm not sure what you expect to happen to us here. I'd be more concerned about our parents getting mad at us for staying out too long."

"Well, there's that too. Whatever the reasons, let's just go home," Phoebe said.

# Chapter IV

Phoebe and Erica started heading back to Adrian's home when Erica pointed something out. It was a flash of light, similar the flash a spark would create.

"Was that lightning?" Erica asked, pointing towards where she saw the light.

Phoebe turned her head. "Was what lightning?"

"That flash. Didn't you see it?" Erica said. "It came from somewhere over there, near that tree." Erica pointed towards a large mulberry tree in full bloom.

"No, I didn't see anything." Phoebe responded. "I highly doubt it would be lightning, though. The sky is clear and I didn't hear any thunder. Plus, the weather report promises clear skies for the rest of the week."

"Hmm, maybe it was my imagination," Erica said.

They continued walking and Erica said, "So, what's going on with your science project? You said it had something to do with filters and water?"

"Well, to put it vaguely, yes." Phoebe said. "I'll put it in terms that make sense to you, but I am basically testing the effectiveness of different household water filters and then documenting my findings. This will help tell what chemicals and minerals work better for filtering water and which ones don't."

"But what about the water?" Erica asked.

"What about it?" Phoebe asked. "The water will be taken straight from the faucet at my house."

"Well, that's my point," Erica said. "You'll only have one type of water going through those filters. Wouldn't it make more sense to use different types of water..." Erica trailed off and started looking in the direction of the bushes.

"What's the matter?" asked Phoebe. "Cat got your tongue?"

"No, it's just that...There!" Erica pointed at another tree, this time at a maple tree. "I swear I saw another flash of light."

"Are you sure?" Phoebe asked, turning around to look at the tree. "I didn't see anything."

"Yes, I'm positive!" Erica said. "It was right over there, near that tree!"

Suddenly, the sound of branches and leaves rustling near the tree could be heard, and soon the sounds of footsteps running.

Erica heard it first and she shouted "Hey, stop! What are you doing?" She took off running after the figure that had just darted out from behind the tree.

"Erica, no, don't," Phoebe called after her, and then sighed. "I hate running," she muttered while chasing after Erica.

The person was running wildly, turning corners and doing basically anything to get away from Erica, but as a midfielder in soccer, Erica had done her fair share of running.

The person shouted over his shoulder, "Stop chasing me! I didn't do anything!"

Erica was now within a few feet of the person, but she couldn't quite reach him. She positioned herself for a perfect football tackle, but suddenly the person ran right into a person walking down the road.

"Oof!" The two people stood up and Erica grabbed the person's wrist. The other person who had been run into stood up.

"Erica? What's going on? Where's Phoebe?" he asked.

"Wait, Scott?" Erica asked, recognizing the voice. "What are you doing here?"

"I take this road as a shortcut to get back home," Scott answered. "What the heck is going on? Who is this person?" he asked.

"Apparently-he-was-spying-on-us," said Phoebe, out-of-breath and breathing heavily.

"Wow, what happened to you?" asked Scott. "You look you just did three rounds with a gorilla."

"I just ran practically a mile," Phoebe panted. "And I hate running. It's such a pointless activity."

Erica rolled her eyes and pulled up the man she was holding by the wrist. Only it wasn't a man. It was a boy about 14 or 15, close in age to Scott.

"What were you doing, hiding in the bushes," Erica demanded. "And were you the one making the flashes?"

"Flashes, hiding in bushes? What's happening?" Scott asked. "Did you guys do something stupid?"

"What? No!" Phoebe protested. "Look, we'll explain later, but let's let Erica do her thing."

Scott shook his head in defeat. "Whatever," he said. "I'm going back home before my parents kill me for being late."

The boy Erica was holding squirmed and twisted his arm, trying to get out of Erica's grasp. "Come on man, just let me go," he pleaded.

Erica narrowed her eyes. "Not until you tell me what you were doing and why you were spying on us."

"Look, I wasn't spying on anybody," the boy said. "Someone paid me 50 bucks to take a photo of you two."

"Someone paid you to take a photo of us," Phoebe asked, confused.

"Yes, exactly," the boy said, squirming. "Now can I go?"

"No. Who paid you to take the photo?" Erica asked.

"I can't tell you. He made me promise I wouldn't mention him. I wasn't even supposed to tell you about him."

Erica pulled on his arm and the boy winced. "Who was it?" she demanded.

"I won't tell you," the boy said, squirming. "I can't."

"Fine," Erica said and started twisting the boy's arm. "Who paid you?"

"Erica, stop! You're hurting him," Phoebe said, sounding concerned. "Don't break his arm!"

The boy was on the verge of crying now. "Stop, please! If I tell you, you have to promise not to tell anyone about me."

"No promises," Erica said, twisting harder. "Who was it?"

"Erica! Stop!" Phoebe grabbed Erica's arm and tried to pull it off of the boy's hand."

"What are you doing!?" asked Erica. "He was stalking us!"

"You're going to damage his arm if you don't stop," Phoebe said. "Just calm down. We can take him down to the police station if he doesn't tell us."

Suddenly the boy's eyes grew wide. "The police? No, please don't take me there!"

Erica relaxed her grip on the boy's arm and the boy sighed with relief.

"Alright, let's take him to the police station." Erica agreed. "I'm sure that they can charge him with stalking or something of the like."

The boy started twisting his arm wildly and tried to break free from Erica's grip. He managed to get his arm free, and tried to run, but Phoebe grabbed his shirt and pulled him back.

"Hey, where do you think you're going?" Erica demanded. "You're staying with us until we get to the police station!"

"Look, don't take me to the police, the boy said. "Just let me go and I promise I'll never come anywhere near you two. Just don't take me to the police."

"Tell me who paid you to take a photo of us, and we'll let you go." Erica said.

The boy looked around desperately and finally said "Okay, fine. I'll tell you."

Erica crossed her arms and tapped her foot. "I'm waiting."

The boy breathed in and said "It was a guy about 25-30. He just came up to me and gave me a camera. He told me that there were two girls walking around the neighborhood and said that he needed a photo of them. He gave me your descriptions and handed me 50 bucks. He said that he trusted that I wouldn't run off with the money and told me to meet him at a certain place."

"What place?" Phoebe asked. "Where did he tell you to meet him."

"I promised that I wouldn't say." The boy said, nervously.

Erica took a step forward and raised her arm threateningly. The boy cowered and raised his arm. "Okay, okay. He told me to meet him at the corner of Rose St. and Maple St."

Erica narrowed her eyes. "How do I know that you aren't lying?" she asked.

"I swear, I'm not!" the boy said. "Just please don't twist my arm anymore."

"And if we do choose to believe you, what time did you say that you would meet him?" Phoebe asked.

"He said to meet him there at 10:30pm."

Erica looked at Phoebe. "Okay...And what's your name."

"Brad," the boy responded. "Brad...Smith."

"Smith? Seriously? How dumb do you think I am?" Erica asked. "What's your real last name?"

"Smith! That's my real last name."

"Fine, whatever." Erica grabbed the boy's camera and let go of the boy's arm and shoved him. The boy ran off and disappeared down the street.

"We should really start heading home." Phoebe stated, checking her watch. "It's almost 10 o clock. Our parents aren't going to be either worried or furious."

"You can go home if you want," Erica said. "I'm going to the address that the boy gave us. I'm going to figure out who wanted a photo of us so desperately."

"What, no. Don't be stupid, Erica." Phoebe sounded exasperated. "Look, if you're that concerned, we can file a report at the police station, but we really need to get home."

"No, the police never take teenagers seriously. Mostly because we're the ones doing the crimes, but still. If we want to catch this person, we have to do it ourselves."

Phoebe sighed. "Come on Erica. We still have to get up for school tomorrow. I'm not staying out until 10pm."

"Go home, then." Erica said, walking away. "I'm going to that address and nothing you say will stop me."

"Erica..." Phoebe said, following her. "This guy could be dangerous. Why is this so important to you, anyway?"

Erica stopped walking. "You mean you don't want to know why some creep is trying to get pictures of us?" she asked. "If you ask me, you're being unreasonable, not me. Now if you don't want to come with me, fine. I'll let you know what happens."

Phoebe sighed. She knew Erica had a point and she didn't want to abandon her, but she also didn't want to stay out until 10:30, trying to catch some stranger, who could possibly be dangerous. Finally, she called out to Erica and said "Fine, I'll come with you. But if this person is armed or looks at all dangerous, we are leaving. Please, please, don't try to fight this person."

Erica turned. "Fine, I promise. I just want to figure out who it is. That's all. Then, we can tell the police."

Phoebe pulled out her phone and texted her parents. "Hey, I'm staying over at Erica tonight. We have a project to work on together. Is that okay?" Then she jogged over to catch up to Erica.

"I told my parents that I was staying over at your house. Aren't your parents going to be concerned when you don't come home soon?" she said.

Erica turned around. "Yeah, but I've stayed out later than this before."

"You have?" Phoebe sounded shocked. "What were you doing?"

"Eh, long story. But it means my parents are used to this. I used to stay out until 11 sometimes, practicing shooting hoops in the dark."

"And your parents didn't care?" Phoebe asked. "Mine would freak out."

"Well, not really. As long as I came back home before midnight and got up for school in the morning, they really weren't very strict. They had their hands full with the twins anyway." Erica said, shrugging.

Phoebe opened her mouth as if to say something, but then closed it again, unable to think of a response.

Meanwhile, Scott was wrapping up the few lines of his essay and getting ready for bed. He was pondering the events of the day when his thoughts turned to Erica and Phoebe. For some reason, what had happened an hour ago hadn't registered in his mind. At least, not how strange it was.

It wasn't until now that he was finally processing what had happened. He started going through all the events in his head and sorting through everything.

"Flashing lights, moving bushes, what the heck happened?" he muttered to himself. "And who was the boy that Erica was holding?"

Scott shut his laptop lid and grabbed his phone. He texted the group chat and asked if Phoebe and Erica had gotten home safely and what the heck had happened with the flashing lights and the boy. The only text he got was from Adrian, asking what was going on.

Scott called Adrian and quickly explained what had happened.

"So, they caught this boy that was taking pictures of them?" Adrian asked, sounding very concerned. "And you just left them?"

"Well, I guess," Scott said. "I didn't really know what else to do. My brain was basically just telling me to get home and finish my essay."

"And you don't know what happened after that?"

"No, I just headed home. I guess I wasn't really thinking." Scott said.

"I'll say!" Adrian responded. "You try calling Phoebe and I'll try calling Erica." Adrian hung up and left Scott staring his phone screen.

Scott dialed Phoebe's number and it started ringing. It rang a few times before Phoebe picked up.

"Hello? Phoebe?" Scott said into the phone. "What's going on?"

"Scott...are...rose...boy." Phoebe was saying something into the phone, but apparently, she had bad connection and her words were cutting out.

"Hello?? I can't hear you, Phoebe." Scott said. "Where are you."

The only things that Scott could pick up from Phoebe's broken call were "maple" and "walking". Then the call cut out and all Scott could hear was the dial tone. He tried calling again, but this time the call went straight to voicemail, most likely because Phoebe no longer had connection.

Instead of calling Phoebe again, Scott called Adrian. "Were you able to talk to Erica?" he asked.

"No, the call didn't go through. Why wouldn't they be home right now?" Adrian asked. "Did Phoebe pick up?"

"Well, she did, but there was really poor signal. I was only able make out a few words."

"What words?" Adrian asked.

"I'm not entirely sure. I think I heard "boy", "rose", "maple", and maybe "walking"? Scott said.

"Well, that doesn't make any sense," Adrian said. "Sounds like she's buying a rose for a boy from a maple tree."

Scott chuckled. "Yeah, I doubt it. But really, this is worrying. It's almost 10:30 and Phoebe and Erica should have been home by now."

"Should we call their parents?" Adrian asked. "That feels like the wise decision in this position."

"No, we don't need to worry them unnecessarily." Scott said. "Besides, I'm sure they told their parents where they were going. They'll probably be back soon."

"Hopefully," Adrian said. "But I really don't understand what Phoebe was trying to say. Maple? Rose? What does that mean?"

"Well, we are certainly missing context, but you're right. I can't think what that would have to do with anything. Maybe Phoebe is doing sort of science project and she roped Erica into helping." Scott suggested.

"Yeah, maybe," Adrian said, and then hung up, once again, leaving Scott staring at his phone screen.

Scott put his phone on his nightstand and grabbed his pajamas. He started changing when something went off in his head. He put his shirt back on and grabbed his phone.

"Rose, maple," he muttered to himself, opening the Maps app. "I knew it!" he exclaimed. He called Adrian who picked up almost instantly and said "I know what Rose and Maple mean!"

"You do? What?" Adrian asked.

"They are street names! Rose Street and Maple Street. There's an intersection that runs right through both of them. That's probably where Phoebe and Erica are!"

"Woah, woah, slow down, Scott." Adrian said. "That's great detective work, but why would they be at this random intersection?"

"I don't know," Scott said, "But it's the only thing that makes sense, given the context. Maybe they chased the boy who was making the flashes and caught him at that intersection. We need to go there!"

"Hang on, how are we supposed to go there?" Adrian asked. "We can't drive, and it's practically 11pm."

"It's only 10:20, and we can bike. It should only take us about 10 minutes."

"Okay, there's so many problems with what you're suggesting," Adrian said. "For starters, you said your bike is broken."

"It is, but I can borrow my dad's bike."

"Okay, and what are we supposed to tell our parents? 'Hey, we're off to some random street intersection to hopefully meet our friends?' Sounds like a plan."

"You don't tell them anything. Haven't you ever climbed out your window?" Scott said.

"What? No! I'm not sneaking out of the house. My parents would kill me!" Adrian said. "Why not just call the police?"

"Because we're just dumb teenagers. They'll assume that Erica and Phoebe are just dumb teenagers sneaking out of the house like all these other reports. They never take these seriously."

"I mean, you're right, but why do we need to go there in the first place? There's no indication of them being in trouble."

"It's 10pm at night and they are at some random intersection. I'm pretty sure that they are in trouble." Scott said, pointedly.

Adrian sighed. "Alright, fine. But you're explaining this to my parents."

"Okay, I'll meet you on Glasgow Road in a minute," Scott answered, sliding open his window.

# Chapter V

Back at the road, Phoebe and Erica had finally reached the intersection. "This place is creepy. This is the back alley of this town," Phoebe said under her breath. She checked her watch and said "It's 10:25, the guy should be here any minute."

Erica took a deep breath. "I'm just going to try to get a look at his face. I won't let him see me and if he has a weapon, I'll ditch."

"Okay, but be careful." Phoebe said. "Weapon or not, he could still be dangerous."

Erica put her finger to her lips. "Shh," she said, pointing towards a person walking out from behind a building. Erica and Phoebe ducked behind a tree to avoid being seen.

"You think that's him?" whispered Phoebe. "He looks about 25-30."

"Of course it's him." Erica whispered back. "I can't see his face, though. It's covered by his hat and hoodie."

The person was wearing a large hooded sweatshirt and a baseball cap pulled down over his face. He stopped walking and looked around, leaning on a nearby tree.

"Well, now what?" whispered Phoebe.

"I need to see his face. Let me get closer." Erica said. "I just want to know who he is."

Erica started inching her way towards the man, being careful to stay hidden. She crouched behind another tree, but still couldn't see his face.

"Erica, you're too close," Phoebe whispered. "He's going to see you."

"I'm fine," Erica whispered. "I still can't see his face, though."

She kept inching closer and closer to the man until – CRACK. Erica stepped on a fallen branch and the man spun around and faced the direction of Phoebe and Erica. Phoebe grabbed Erica and pulled her down, behind a bunch of bushes.

"Don't make a sound," Phoebe breathed. "Let's hope he doesn't see us."

The man started walking closer and closer to Phoebe and Erica. He started peering around behind trees and looking in the bushes. Suddenly he put his hand in his pocket and took a large pocket knife out.

Erica let out a stifled gasp, and Phoebe quickly put her hand over Erica's mouth, but it was too late. The man walked over to where Phoebe and Erica were hiding and started to move the bushes aside. He didn't get very far when Erica leaped out of the bushes and tackled the man.

"Erica!" Phoebe shouted and jumped out of the bushes. Erica was trying to pin the man to the ground, but he was clearly stronger than her. He was able to force Erica off of him, and stood up. Erica got to her feet, but the man was faster. He aimed a kick at Erica, and caught her in the side. Erica cried out, and struggled to her feet while the man aimed another kick. This time, she was able to roll out of the way, and get to her feet.

She clutched her side and ducked as the man tried to punch her. She landed a hard elbow to his rib and fast punch to his chin. The man grunted and charged at Erica, shoving her to the ground, hard. Erica felt blood on her head as she tried to force the man off of her. The man punched Erica in the jaw, picked her up off the ground by her arm and flung her against a tree. He was about to grab Erica again when Phoebe jumped on the man's back, clawing at his neck.

The man tried to shake Phoebe off, but she clung on with a death grip. He was finally able to pull her hands off his neck, and shoved her off. However, this gave Erica enough time to recover herself and give the man a swift kick in the stomach. The man doubled over, and Erica raised her fist. Instead of raising his head, the man headbutted Erica in the chest, knocking her to the ground again. Breathing heavily, he grabbed his pocket knife off the ground where Erica had knocked it out of his hand. He started towards to Erica and slashed his knife at her.

Erica ducked and grabbed his wrist, attempting to force him to drop his knife. Instead, the man kicked Erica in the ankle and either inadvertently or purposefully slashed her in the arm as she fell. He was about to stab her again when Scott and Adrian charged in with their bikes. Scott hit his brakes and dove off his bike, tackling the man and knocking the knife out of his grip. Like Erica, Scott attempted to pin the man, but he managed to break free from Scott's grip and punch him in the nose.

Scott staggered back and the man got to his feet and took off running. Adrian tore after him on his bike, but the man jumped into a grey pickup truck and tore down the road. Knowing there was no way to catch him, Adrian biked back to the group.

Phoebe was picking herself off the ground, dazed, but for the most part, unhurt. Scott's nose was bleeding, and he had some scratches on his arms and legs, but nothing serious. Erica however, was badly injured.

Scott ran over to Erica who was leaning against a tree and looked at her injuries. There was a cut on the back of her head, which was still bleeding, as well as a deep cut on her arm from the knife, which was bleeding as well. There were other minor injuries, including many bruises, scrapes and cuts, but the cut on her arm and head were by far the worst.

"Erica, are you okay?" Scott asked. He turned to Phoebe. "What in the world just happened here."

Phoebe looked at Scott and raised her hands in defeat. "Honestly, I have no idea anymore."

Erica winced and put her hand on the back of her head. "That hurts," she said. "Where did he go?"

"He got away," said Adrian. "I chased him with my bike, but he drove off in a pickup truck."

Erica punched the ground. "Of course he did. At least I got a good look at his face." She tried to stand up, "We need to go to the police station!"

Erica winced in pain and sat back down again. "My ankle hurts. I don't think I can walk," she said through gritted teeth. "It might be broken."

Scott rolled up her pant leg and looked at her ankle. It looked swollen and bruised, but he couldn't tell whether or not it was broken. Phoebe walked over and said "Let me see." She looked at Erica's ankle and touched a few spots. Each time she did, Erica winced. "Ow, stop," she said. "Does anyone have a first-aid kit?"

Scott, Adrian, and Phoebe all shook their heads. "Great," Erica moaned. "How am I supposed to get to the police station?"

"We might not be able to do anything about your ankle right now, but we can stop the bleeding on your arm and head," Phoebe said. "Scott, can pass me that knife?" Phoebe gestured to the man's knife which he had dropped. Scott grabbed the knife and Erica eyes grew wide.

"What are you going to do with that?" she asked.

"Calm down," Phoebe said. "I just need to cut off a strip of fabric. Adrian, can you cut two strips off your shirt?"

Phoebe handed him the knife and he cut some of his sift off and gave it to Phoebe. "Good thing I didn't wear my favorite shirt," he said.

Phoebe took the two strips and tied them around Erica's cuts. "This will help stop the bleeding and reduce the possibility of an infection," she said. "We need to get you home now, though."

"No, we need to go to the police station," Erica said. "We need to report this and tell them who to look for."

"Erica, you can barely walk. The police station is 10 miles from here. You'll never make it." Adrian said. "The best option now is to get home and get a first-aid kit."

"How are we supposed to get home?" Erica asked. "Phoebe and my bikes are parked over at Mr. McGinnis' house. Besides, I don't think I can bike anyway."

"Oh yeah, our bikes!" Phoebe slapped herself in the forehead. "I completely forgot about them. Why did we walk here? We should have biked."

"We'll have to get our parents," Scott said. "My dad has a truck and he can come pick us up."

"How are we supposed to explain what happened to our parents?" Adrian asked. "They'll freak out."

"That's probably the least of our worries," said Phoebe, looking at Erica. "Right now, we just need to get cleaned up and get Erica's injuries dressed. Scott, call your dad. Ask him to pick us up."

Scott took his phone out of his pocket and dialed his dad's number. "There's no signal here," he said. "We have to get out of this back alley."

"Okay, you go with Adrian to find a place where there's cell signal," Phoebe said. "I'll stay with Erica."

Scott nodded and hopped on his bike. Adrian followed suit and they biked out of the alley, with Scott checking for phone signal.

"You know, that was some really good fighting," Phoebe said to Erica. "Where did you learn to fight like that?"

"What, you mean getting my butt kicked," Erica laughed, and then winced. "Ouch, my side hurts when I laugh."

"Well, he did give you a pretty hard kick there," said Phoebe. "I'm impressed that you held your own for that long."

"You jumping on him might have saved my life, though. It managed to delay him long enough to give time for Scott and Adrian to get here. He might have stabbed me if not for you."

Phoebe looked at Erica's arm. "Does that hurt?" she asked.

"Yeah, it hurts a lot, actually. Especially when I raise my arm. I've been hurt worse, though. You should have seen me after the ice hockey tournament in Colorado a few years ago," Erica said, biting her tongue.

Scott and Adrian's bikes came back down the alley and Scott hopped off his. "My dad's coming to get us. I told him where we were. He completely panicked, but he said he'll be there in a few minutes."

"I'm sure I can expect to get a fun lecture from my dad," said Adrian. "I've never snuck out before and I've never been out this late before."

"We're probably all going to get lectures plus who knows what else," replied Scott. "However, while we wait for my dad, can somebody *please* explain to me what just went down here."

"Where should I start?" asked Phoebe?"

"Try the beginning," Adrian said. "At least I'll have an actual reason for breaking the rules."

"Okay, but I might not be able to finish." Phoebe said.

"Well, condense it a bit. Just please enlighten me!" Scott said, exasperated.

Phoebe shrugged and said "Okay, but you're going to think it's ridiculous."

"Just tell me!"

"Well, basically some kid was taking pictures of me and Erica. Erica found out that someone paid him 50 bucks to take the picture. He gave us an address that he said he would meet the buyer at. So Erica forced me to come along to that address and figure out who this person was. We saw the man, but he noticed us hiding and basically attacked us. Although, I will say that Erica started the fight, but he was probably going to attack us once he found us anyway."

Phoebe took a deep breath, "Yeah, that's basically what happened, give or take a few details."

"Wow, that's something," said Adrian. "And all this started because some idiot ran over my flower garden. Geez Erica, I'm really sorry about this. I wouldn't have asked for you guy's help if I had known something like this would happen."

"It's not your fault," said Erica, "Besides, we pretty much volunteered to help you; you didn't really ask us."

"Still, it was my garden that started this whole "adventure"," Adrian said.

"Look Adrian, nobody is blaming anybody for what happened here," Scott said. "Everything is okay, just as long as we get home safely and nobody is too badly hurt."

"Well, I won't be playing sports for a while," said Erica. "I hope I don't get too rusty."

Suddenly they saw the headlights of a car approaching and they all shielded their eyes.

"Scott, Adrian, Erica, Phoebe?" a man's voice called out.

"Dad! Over here!" Scott called out.

Scott's dad pulled his truck up next to Scott. "What in the world are you guys doing out here at 11pm at night?" he asked.

"It's a long story, Dad," Scott said. "We'll explain when we get home."

Scott's dad sighed. "Alright, hop in," he said. "Erica, Scott told me that you hurt your ankle. Can you walk?"

"No, I don't think so," Erica replied, trying to stand up. "Nope, definitely not."

Scott's dad stepped out of the car. "Okay, hang on. Let me carry you over to the truck." He bent down and picked up Erica, carrying her over to the truck. She pulled herself onto one of the seats, gritting her teeth. Scott's dad looked at Erica's ankle and clicked his tongue.

"That's a nasty break," he said. "We should get you to the ER. I'll contact your parents. Yours too," he said, gesturing to Adrian and Phoebe.

"I'm okay," said Erica. "There's no need to take me to the ER."

Scott's dad shook his head. "This isn't up for debate. If we don't get you to the ER now, it could get much worse."

He grabbed Scott and Adrian's bikes and tossed them into the truck bed. "Where are your bikes?" he asked Erica and Phoebe.

"We left them in front of Mr. McGinnis' house, said Phoebe.

"Okay, I'll pick them up on the way." Scott dad's started the truck and backed out of the alley. "You really owe me a big explanation," he said, looking at Scott."

"Yes, I know, Dad," Scott replied. "Adrian and I were just trying to help Phoebe and Erica. That's why I snuck out."

"I guess it's a good thing that you did. But what were you two doing out at 11pm in the first place?" Scott's dad asked, looking at Erica and Phoebe.

"Would you do the honors?" Phoebe asked Erica. "I've already told this story once."

"Sure," Erica said. She then related the story to Scott's dad, doing her best to not omit any key details.

Scott's dad nodded. "Sounds like a classic case of a creep being creepy, to put it lightly," he said. "But Erica, you should know better than to try and track down somebody like this. For all you knew, he could have had a gun. You're lucky that you got away with nothing more than a broken ankle and some cuts. And Scott, what happened to your nose?"

Scott told his dad about how the man had punched him in the nose and shoved him away.

Scott's dad nodded again. "You may have saved Erica's life," he said. "Who knows what he was going to do with that knife."

"Oh yeah, I almost forgot." Adrian produced the knife that the man had dropped. "This might help the police catch the man who attacked us."

Scott's dad whistled. "That's a big knife for a pocketknife," he said. "The police should be able to track the serial number on it, though. Good work, Adrian."

He pulled the car over next to Mr. McGinnis' house and pointed at the two bikes parked out in front. "Those yours?" he asked. Phoebe nodded and Scott put the two bikes into the truck bed.

"Scott, Adrian, and Phoebe. You guys don't need to come with us to the ER. I'm going to drop you off at your home, and then drive Erica to the ER. I told her parents to meet me there," Scott's dad said.

The kids nodded and Scott's dad started the truck up again. He dropped Phoebe off first, then Adrian, and then Scott. Scott waved, and his dad drove the truck off again.

After explaining everything to all their parents and getting the respective lectures that they all knew were coming, all the kids finally went to bed.

# Chapter VI

Scott awoke to the jarring sound of his alarm clock. He turned over and rubbed his eyes. "Is it 7 already?" he muttered to himself.

He rolled out of bed and changed into school clothes, forgetting to comb his hair or make his bed. He headed downstairs, where he saw Greg on his laptop, browsing lists of colleges.

"Hey sleepyhead," Greg said to Scott as he walked by. Scott grunted in response and poured himself a cup of orange juice. "Where's Mom and Dad?" he asked.

"They left early for the store," said Greg. "They wanted to get an early start on the day."

"Cool." Scott gulped down his cup of orange juice and grabbed a carton of eggs. "Did they leave any messages for me?"

"Nope." Greg closed his laptop lid. "What the heck happened to you last night. You came home with a bloody nose at almost midnight with some ridiculous story about some stalker."

"Ridiculous?" asked Scott, cracking an egg into a bowl. "How's it ridiculous?"

"Oh, come on," said Greg. "You really expect me to believe that story? What *really* happened?"

Scott rolled his eyes and dumped the eggs into a pan. "What do you think happened?" he asked Greg.

Greg shrugged. "No clue, but not whatever you said." He opened his laptop again, and started browsing the list of college again. Scott served the eggs onto a plate and started gobbling them down. After he finished, he grabbed his backpack and headed out the door.

"I'm going to school," he told Greg, and shut the door behind him. Greg didn't even bother to look up from his laptop.

Scott walked to school where he met Adrian and Phoebe. "Did you hear anything about Erica from your dad?" Adrian asked.

"Nope, he left before I got up," Scott answered. "I hope she's okay."

"Hi!" a voice called out from behind Scott. It was Erica, holding a soccer ball and a piece of paper. She had a cast on her ankle and a bandage on her arm.

"Erica! Hi! We all thought you wouldn't be in school today." Scott said, as Erica walked up to them. She was limping a little bit, but she seemed mostly fine.

Erica smiled. "Well, I wasn't going to be, but then I remembered that today is the day where we get new players for the soccer teams. I might not be able to play, but as the captain, I have to at least welcome the new players."

"How's your ankle," Adrian asked. "Was it broken?"

"No, I just twisted it," Erica said. "The doctor said I should wear the cast for a few weeks, but I shouldn't need crutches. He just said not to put too much strain on it for a while."

"What about your arm?" asked Phoebe. "The cut looked pretty bad."

"Doctor said it was nothing to worry about. He put a bandage on it and said to replace it every few days. As long as we keep it covered, it should heal up nicely. It still stings a little, but not nearly as much as it did before."

"And your head?" asked Scott.

"That needed 3 staples," said Erica. "Once again, the doctor said not to do anything strenuous for a few weeks, and then we can get the staples removed. It should heal up like a normal cut as well."

"Well, I'm glad that there was nothing too serious," said Adrian. "My parents brought the knife to the police station last night and explained what happened. They said the police might ask to see us after school."

Suddenly the bell rang and Scott said "Shoot, let's get to class. I'll see all you guys later." Scott and the rest of the group dashed off to their respective classes.

Adrian was sitting in Algebra II when it happened. A police officer knocked on the classroom door and asked to see an Adrian Curtis. Adrian raised his hand and said "That's me." The office asked Adrian to follow him, which Adrian did (while the entire class gawked). He walked outside, where he saw Phoebe, Erica, and Scott.

The officer said "Just make sure we're clear, you aren't in trouble. We just want to ask a couple of questions. Will you come to the police station with me?"

The kids all nodded at the same time, and the officer gestured for them to follow him. The followed him into the police car, and he drove them to the station, where he told them to sit in a room, with chairs and a table.

"Wait here," he said. "I'll be right back."

They all took seats and looked around. "Wow. They didn't even wait for school to end," said Scott.

Adrian chuckled. "Well, I guess that's a good thing. After all, it shows that they care about their job. Plus, Algebra II is boring."

"Hey, at least you weren't doing Biology." said Erica. "Last thing I want to do is cut up frog legs."

"I, for one, would have liked to finish my class," said Phoebe. "Trig is very important, and I need to be as prepared as possible if I want to pass the SAT with a perfect score."

Scott laughed. "My dad always told me that it wasn't necessarily about how well I did, as long as I tried my best."

Phoebe looked astonished. "That's a horrible way of thinking. If your best can only give you a 97% on a test, that means you have to study more and make your best even better."

Erica shook her head. "Not everyone loves schoolwork as much as you do," she said.

Phoebe was about to say something, but the door opened and an officer walked in. His brow was glistening with sweat and he had brown hair with a scruffy brown mustache. He nodded his head in greeting and shut the door. He took a seat at the table, across from where the kids were sitting.

"My name is Officer McKinley. So, as you might have been told, I just want to ask you some questions about what happened and who attacked you last night," the officer said. "Is that okay with you?"

They all nodded and the officer gave a thumbs-up. "Good," he said. "Now, just answer as well as you can. If you aren't sure about something, just say so."

The officer opened a clipboard and flipped a couple of pages. "So, first off, I'd like to start with a basic description. Erica, that's your name, right?" he asked, pointing his pen at her.

Erica nodded. "Yep, that's me."

"Great. Now, from what your parents tell me, you most likely got the closet look at the attacker, since you were the one he attacked. Do you remember what his face looked like?"

Erica bunched her eyebrows. "Well, honestly, I wasn't really paying attention to his face. I was more trying to dodge his kicks and punches. But from what I can remember, he had dark, black hair. I think he had a mole on his forehead, but that could have been dirt."

"Anything else you can remember?" the officer asked.

Erica shook her head. "Sorry, it was dark, and like I said, I really wasn't paying attention to his face."

"No, that's okay," the officer responded. Then her turned to the rest of the kids. "Anybody else remember anything about how the man looked?"

Scott scratched his head. "He was pretty tall; about 6ft 4" he said.

"Okay, that's good," the officer said, writing on his clipboard. "Anybody else?"

The kids all shook their heads. The officer flipped another page on his clipboard and said, "What about what he was wearing? Any noticeable clothing, or strange outfits?"

Phoebe closed her eyes. "He had on a black hoodie with the words 'Shark Life' written on it, along with a picture of a shark. The hoodie was mostly covering his face, but he also had on a baseball cap with the Raiders logo on it. The hat fell off in the fight, but he grabbed it before he ran off. He had a grey pair of sweatpants with the Nike logo on the side and heavy-duty boots. The boots were yellow and black with grey laces."

Erica, Adrian, and Scott stared at Phoebe. "How do you remember all that?" Scott asked. "I can barely remember what I wore yesterday.

"I have a photographic memory, remember?" said Phoebe. "I can basically visualize anything that happened to me."

"Wow, that's awesome," said Erica. "I'm like Scott, though. I don't even remember what I had for lunch yesterday."

"Chicken nuggets and a Caeser salad," said Phoebe.

"Well, it's a good thing that you have that ability," said the officer. "That will be very helpful in catching the criminal."

"Wouldn't he have changed his clothes by now?" asked Adrian. "I mean, this happened yesterday."

"Yes, but we would be able to comb through all security footage from home, stores, smart cars, etc..." the officer responded. "We'll match anyone wearing that outfit, and find his identity."

"Well, of course," said Phoebe. "That's why there are so many cameras in cities like NYC. There's so much crime there, but most of the criminals get caught, simply because they were caught on tape."

"Speaking of cameras," Erica broke in, digging through her backpack. "I also have this." She pulled out the camera that she had taken from the boy who had taken the photo of her and Phoebe earlier.

"What is this?" the officer asked.

"Did my Dad tell you how we came across this person in the first place?" asked Erica.

"No, actually," the officer answered. "He said that he wasn't entirely sure how it happened in the first place. I was going to ask you about that shortly."

"So basically..." Erica proceeded to explain the whole story about meeting the boy, taking the camera, and going to the address.

The officer nodded again for the third time. "So, from what I understand, he sent someone to take a photo of you two, and after getting an address from that person, you decided to go to that address and find the person who sent the boy after you, knowing that he could be dangerous."

"Well, when you put it like that..." Erica said, hesitatingly.

"I'm sure you understand that what you did was very foolish and dangerous," the officer said. "Why didn't you just report this to the police right away?"

"Well...I was worried that you wouldn't take us seriously," said Erica. "I've heard that police don't often listen to teenagers."

The officer shook his head. "We take all calls seriously. Especially ones about stalkers."

"Sorry," said Erica meekly.

The officer sighed. "It's okay." He flipped his clipboard up and said "That's all the questions I have for you. I'll have another officer bring you back to school."

"Thanks," said Adrian. "Oh yeah, one more thing. The man drives a grey pickup truck. He drove away in it after Scott and I showed up."

"Did you get the license number?" the officer asked, opening his clipboard again.

Adrian shook his head. "Sorry, it was dark and he drove away too fast."

"It's fine," said the officer. "You all have been a lot of help."

The officer escorted them to the exit where they got into another police car with an officer. The officer drove them back to school. Scott and Adrian headed off to their world history class, Phoebe to her geometry class, and Erica to her physics class.

After school, Scott headed to the music room where he sometimes went after school. It was a nice, quiet place to practice his guitar, plus there was lots of sheet music there. And he really liked the guitar that they had there.

Scott opened the door to the room and stepped in. He walked over to the guitar and picked it up. He was about to start playing when he heard someone say "Hi Scott."

Startled, Scott whirled around and saw Erica sitting in the corner, near the drums.

"Erica. Geez, you nearly gave me a heart attack. What are you doing here?" Scott asked.

"Well, normally I would be practicing softball, but since I can't run, I figured I might as well practice drums. I haven't played them in a while, anyway," Erica answered.

"Wow, I completely forgot that you played the drums," said Scott. "How long have you been playing for again?"

"6 years, I think," said Erica. She picked up a drumstick and started half-heartedly playing a slow rhythm.

"Is something wrong?" asked Scott. "You seem like you're thinking about something."

"No, everything's fine," Erica answered.

"Erica...We've been friends since kindergarten. I can tell when something is the matter," Scott said.

Erica sighed. "You're right," she said, putting down her drumsticks. "Why am I so stupid sometimes!?" she asked.

"How do you mean?" asked Scott.

"Well, look at me. My ankle is sprained and I needed to get staples because I wouldn't listen to Phoebe's advice. Instead of going to the police, I just *had* to figure out who this person was myself."

"You've always wanted to take things into your own hands," said Scott. "It's not necessarily a bad thing. I mean, look on the bright side. If you and Phoebe hadn't went to that address, the police wouldn't even have a description or any way of catching that creep."

"Yeah, but my ankle wouldn't be sprained, and I'd be playing softball right now instead of playing these stupid drums." Erica said, frustrated. "Plus, I put Phoebe in danger as well. If you and Adrian hadn't shown up when you did, he might have stabbed me with that pocketknife."

"Look, I understand," said Scott. "You were worried about your safety and mad that some creep was trying to take pictures of you. You might not have made the best decisions, but you had good intent."

"What's the point in having good intent if all you do is put your friends in danger?" Erica asked. "I didn't even catch the guy, I just got beat up by him. Heck, I'm surprised Phoebe hasn't said 'I told you so' already. I wouldn't blame her if she was mad at me."

"Erica, stop beating yourself up over this," said Scott. "Phoebe's not mad at you, and neither is anybody else. Look, what you need is a distraction. Something to take your mind off what happened."

"A distraction? Like what, sports? I can't exactly do that anymore, can I?" Erica said.

"No, not sports, but how about what you're doing now? Music is a great distraction." Scott said, picking up his guitar.

"That's what I was trying, but I just can't seem to concentrate. I keep thinking about what happened, and how it was my fault," Erica answered.

"Well, then why don't we go back to what we were doing originally and try to help Adrian figure out who ran over his garden?" Scott suggested.

"That's what got us into this in the first place," Erica said.

"No, the creep taking a picture of you and Phoebe was what got us into this in the first place. Adrian's garden had nothing to do with that."

"I guess you're right..." Erica picked up her drumstick and started playing a slow drum solo. "We can go to Adrian's house in a bit and see if we can find anything new."

Scott started playing his guitar along to the beat of Erica's drums. "Hey, we could play duets. We sound pretty good together!"

Erica laughed. "Yeah, maybe this could become an after-school thing."

"Hey, doesn't Phoebe play piano?" Scott asked, strumming on his guitar. "Maybe we could start a band."

"What about Adrian?" Erica asked. "I don't think he plays an instrument."

"Hmm, you're right," said Scott. "Well, I guess he can be lead vocalist."

Erica grinned. "Adrian? Sing? Somehow I can't picture that no matter how hard I try."

"Hey, you never know! Maybe he has a really good voice."

Scott and Erica played a few more duets for about half an hour when Scott said "I should get home. I have a lot of homework to do; I think the teachers are giving us more and more homework as Summer break gets closer."

Erica chuckled and then said "Alright, see you later. I'll see if we can all coordinate a time to meet at Adrian's house."

Scott arrived at home in a few minutes to find his parents sitting at the dining room table, looking through what appeared to be video footage. "What's going on?" Scott asked.

"It's the strangest thing ever," Scott's dad said. "We're missing a chunk of video footage from our store's security camera."

"Which camera?" asked Scott. Scott's parents had recently upgraded their security system after someone had broken into the store and made off with the money in the cash register.

"The outside camera that's pointed at the parking lot," answered Scott's dad. "And only that one, too. All the other cameras have all their footage."

"What's missing from it?" Scott asked.

"The footage from 1pm to 2pm is missing." Scott's mom answered. "A woman had her car parked in our parking lot, and when she went to put her groceries in her car, she noticed a huge dent in it. She said that someone had probably hit her car, so we looked at the footage from our camera from the time that she was parked there, but the footage was gone."

"That *is* strange," said Scott. "Could it have been a hardware problem?"

"Well, I suppose it could have been," said Scott's dad, "But these are new cameras. I can't believe that one of them would fail so soon. And it seems like such a coincidence that it happened at the time that someone's car was hit."

"What are you suggesting?" asked Scott.

"I don't know. It seems ridiculous, but it almost feels like someone deleted the footage or stopped the camera from recording."

"How would they go about doing that?" said Scott.

"I don't know, but short of a hardware problem mixed with a lot of coincidence, that's the only thing that I can think of."

Scott shrugged his shoulders and grabbed his bag, heading off to do his homework. He pulled open his laptop when his phone vibrated. He checked his text, when he saw a text from Erica to the group chat. It read: "You guys are never going to believe what my dad told me!"

A text from Adrian popped up: "What did he say?"

Erica texted "Too much to explain over text. I'll explain when we meet at Adrian's house later. What time do you want to meet?"

Scott texted "Does 5:30 work?"

Erica, Phoebe and Adrian all sent thumbs-up, so Scott put his phone on the desk and turned back to his desk. His essay was due tomorrow, so he decided he'd get that done first. He opened up his essay, but for whatever reason, he simply couldn't concentrate on it. He sat there for 10 minutes and typed 1 sentence. Scott shut his laptop lid and decided he'd come back to the essay.

He grabbed "The Call of the Wild", his assigned reading off his desk, and plopped down on his bed to read the assigned chapter. Once again, he couldn't concentrate. Frustrated, Scott grabbed his guitar and started strumming random chords in an attempt to clear his head. Then it hit Scott.

Erica and Phoebe had said that the camera that the person they visited owned had missing footage as well. He knew that there was something bothering him and preventing him from concentrating. He knew there had to be some connection, especially since the footage that was missing from both cameras was footage that was actually needed.

Now that he had figured out what was bothering him, Scott was finally able to concentrate more on his homework. He finished his essay, and the remainder of the time before he was supposed to go to Adrian's house flew by.

It was 5:15 and Scott headed into the kitchen for a snack before he had to leave for Adrian's house. His parents were gone, but the left a note on the fridge telling him that they had gone back to the store. Greg was out hunting for jobs, so there was nobody to drive him. Scott grabbed an apple from the fridge and chomped down on it.

Scott finished the apple and headed outside. He looked at the time and decided he did not want to walk to Adrian's house. So, he grabbed his Dad's bike and pedaled away. He arrived a Adrian's house at the same time as Phoebe and Erica got there on a Segway about a minute later.

Adrian stepped out of his house and asked Erica "So, what's this big news that you wanted to tell us about? And where did you get that thing you're riding?"

Erica leaned her Segway against a tree and said "Well, my parents bought it used a few months ago. It was cheap, but they never ride it, so they said I was free to use it, since I can't exactly ride my bike. Anyway, you remember how my sister, Penelope's car was stolen?"

"Yeah...," said Adrian. "Why?"

"Well, it turns out a neighbor had a security camera that actually faces the road where Penelope's car was stolen from. But-"

"Wait, let me guess," said Scott. "The footage for the time that the car was stolen is missing."

"Yes, exactly!" Erica said. "Exactly what happened when we tried to get footage from that guy who lives near Adrian."

"The same thing happened to my parents at their store." Scott explained what his parents had told him.

"There's no way all these things are coincidences," said Adrian. "There's no way three cameras can fail right at crucial times."

"I agree," said Phoebe. "Someone must be doing something to these cameras to prevent them from recording. Or perhaps they are deleting the footage."

"But how?" asked Adrian. "I didn't think that was even possible."

"Well, all these cameras are connected to the internet, I assume," said Phoebe.

"My parents' camera was," answered Scott. "It uploads the footage onto a drive in my parents' computer."

"So was the man who we visited's camera," said Erica. "And I think my sister's camera was as well."

"Well then all someone would have to do is hack into the camera's control panel and either stop it from recording, or re-route the places where the footage is being uploaded. Or they could hack into the computer where the footage is stored, and delete it from there. I think the first one would be simpler, though," Phoebe finished.

"That sounds like a lot of work," said Adrian. "Why go through all that trouble."

"Actually," Scott broke in, "For someone who's experienced in hacking, it really wouldn't be that much trouble. Ironically, security cameras rarely have anything above basic password protection. So, all a person would have to do is crack a password, and they can do whatever they want with the camera."

"Shouldn't there be another copy of the footage somewhere?" asked Erica. "Doesn't the camera store it's data in its own hard drive?"

"Security cameras rarely have much space in them. Especially not the ones that upload the footage to somewhere else. They usually upload the footage and then delete it later," Phoebe said.

"So, basically, there's someone who's stealing cars and then hacking the cameras that might have caught them stealing the car." Adrian said.

"Wait a minute," said Erica. "When Phoebe and I went that Adrian's neighbor's house, we weren't trying to find footage of the stolen car. We were trying to find footage of the car that drove over Adrian's garden."

"And since the footage was erased, that probably means that it was the same car that was stolen from Old Man McGinnis and drove over Adrian's garden," said Scott.

"What about your parent's store?" asked Phoebe. "Why did the thief erase the footage from there?"

"The person who hit the car in the parking lot must have been driving a stolen car," Scott said.

"Yeah, but whose?" asked Erica. "There haven't been any cars stolen recently."

"Well, not necessarily," said Adrian. "I overheard the P.E. teacher talking to the chemistry teacher. He was saying that his car might have been stolen."

"Might have?" asked Scott. "What does he mean by that?"

"Well, apparently his son keeps "borrowing" his car and sometimes he doesn't return it for days at a time, so he's not sure if that's what happened now, or if someone actually stolen," Adrian answered. "But I'm betting that it was his car that was stolen and the thief probably drove it into the car in your parking lot."

"But the timing's not right," said Phoebe. "If was talking about his car being stolen while he was at school, that means it was probably stolen before school. And you said that the footage missing from your parent's camera was from around 1pm to 2pm., which means that the car would have been stolen while he was a school, and he wouldn't have known about it until after he came home."

"Not really," said Erica. "The P.E. teacher lives 5 minutes away from school. Sometimes he goes home to get some equipment from his house in the middle of school. And you'd know that if you went to P.E., Phoebe."

Phoebe's Literature class was held during P.E., which meant that she got a free pass to skip P.E. Since none of them liked P.E., including Erica, they were all slightly jealous that Phoebe got to skip P.E.

Phoebe ignored this comment and said "There's one thing, though. How does the thief always know exactly where the cameras are? I mean, how does he always know exactly which cameras to hack and delete?"

"Well, that means he probably scouts out the place near where he steals the car and locates all the security cameras," said Scott. "He's very dedicated to his theft, I guess."

"So, basically we have someone who is stealing all the cars in the neighborhood, and the police have no idea who it is, since he erases all trace of him," said Erica. "That's fantastic."

A police car suddenly pulled up in front of Adrian's house where the group was standing, and Officer McKinley stepped out. He gestured for them to come over, and they all walked over.

"Your parents told me that you would be here. I'm afraid I have some rather distressing news," McKinley said. "I had my officers go through the area where you were attacked and track down all the footage from security cameras near the area that could have potentially caught the attacker."

"And all the footage was erased, right?" asked Erica.

McKinley looked surprised. "Yes, exactly," he said. "How did you-?"

Erica and Scott proceeded to tell him about how all the cars had been stolen and the footage had been erased.

After they had finished, McKinley scratched his head. "I see you've heard about the car thefts and the erased footage," he said. "Yeah, we've been working on those cases for a while, but we've hit nothing but dead ends."

"You don't think that these two events could be related, do you?" asked Adrian.

"Well, I don't know," McKinley answered, opening his car door again. "It seems like it, based on the fact that the security camera footage was erased, but I can't see any connection between a creep/stalker and a car thief." McKinley got into his car and said "I have to get back to the station to piece together what little clues we have. Be careful; you never know when the stalker will come back."

The officer drove away, and Phoebe, Scott, Erica, and Adrian all looked at each other. "So, what do you think?" asked Scott.

"I'm not sure," said Erica. "On one hand, it seems like the crimes are related, but then I think about it more and realize that there's no real connection."

"What if the stalker is the car thief?" suggested Adrian. "Maybe he was concerned that you two were getting in his way when you were trying to figure out who ran over my garden and he tried to scare you off."

"But why hire someone to take a picture of us?" Phoebe asked. "Surely there must be better ways of scaring us off."

"I'm not even sure what to think anymore!" said Adrian. "All I know is that I'm probably not getting the money for my garden back."

"Not necessarily," said Erica. "If the police catch the thief, maybe they can make him pay you back."

"That's *if* they even catch the thief," said Adrian. "The guy is a hacker and a car thief. I don't think the cops have much of a chance. They don't even have a clue about who this guy could be."

"Wait a minute," said Scott. "They might not have a clue, but we do!"

"What are you talking about?" asked Phoebe. "What clue?"

"Adrian and I found a quarter that someone dropped in his garden and I took a fingerprint off of it," Scott said. He took the quarter off the counter where they had left it. "We think it might belong to the person was driving the stolen car."

Adrian cleared his throat. "You mean that *you* think it might belong to the person driving the stolen car."

"What? You don't agree with me?" asked Scott.

Adrian shrugged. "I dunno. It just doesn't seem likely. How did it get there in the first place? The guy was driving, not walking."

"Okay, so I've thought about that," said Scott. "Here's my idea of what happened. So, the guy steals the car from Mr. McGinnis. He drives like a maniac or something down the street, swerves and drives over Adrian's garden. Realizing that he hit something, he stops the car and gets out. He leans down to inspect Adrian's garden and view the damage that he's done, and the quarter falls out of his pocket. He then takes off again, not noticing the quarter."

"Well, that's a great theory, but it's pointless," Erica broke in. "Assuming that this quarter does belong to him, how do you intend to match the fingerprint on it to someone? It's not like you have a record of everyone's fingerprints."

"Well, I haven't quite figured out that part yet," said Scott. "But it's a start, right?"

"Barely," muttered Erica.

"Well," said Phoebe. "There's a simple way to catch this person that we are overlooking."

"We're listening," said Scott.

"So, the thief is able to hack security cameras and delete footage to hide the fact that he was ever there, right? So, all we need is a security camera that isn't connected to the internet. That way, he can't hack it, and we'll be able to retrieve the footage."

"Okay, but if he sees a security camera and realizes that he can't hack it, he just won't steal the car, right?" Adrian asked. "I doubt he's that stupid."

"We don't need him to steal the car. We just to get him on camera," Phoebe answered. "Just look for suspicious person that seems to be checking out the place. Once he sees the camera, he'll probably leave, but his face will still be on camera."

"That's...actually a great idea," said Erica. "The only problem is that we don't know where the person is going to steal the car from. What house do we put the security camera at?"

"Not sure yet," said Phoebe. "We need to figure out the thief's MO."

"MO?" asked Scott.

"Modus Operandi," said Phoebe. "It's Latin for Mode of Operation. It means how he plans out his crimes."

"That's easy," said Adrian. "He steals cars and then wipes all footage of him off nearby cameras."

"Well, yes, but what kind of cars does he steal?" Phoebe asked. "It's less about what crimes he commits and more about how he chooses where and when to commit his crimes."

"I don't think that he actually goes for expensive cars," said Erica. "My sister's car was not expensive; I remember my parents buying it for her. They bought it for a couple thousand dollars from a used-car lot."

"So, we are back to square one," said Scott. "Why don't we just leave this up to the police? It's their job after all, isn't it?"

"I suppose so." Phoebe sighed. "I'm just concerned that he'll steal one of our cars next. My parents only have 1 car, and they can't afford to get a new one."

"Wouldn't insurance cover car theft?" Adrian asked.

"Normally, but the insurance provided by my dad's job kind of stinks," Phoebe said. "It only covers damage from accidents."

Scott clicked his tongue. "That sucks," he said. "I don't think the thief will come after our cars, though. There's usually someone home, right?"

"Well, usually my mom is home when I'm not," said Adrian. "Since Katie is homeschooled, someone has to stay home to watch her, and since Dad works, it's usually my mom. Sometimes when I get home from school, I'll watch her, though."

"Yeah, my mom doesn't work," said Erica. "Teddy and Lucy are old enough to be left home alone, but she just stays home and cooks, since there's not really anywhere to go."

"Same thing for me, I guess," said Phoebe. "What about you?" she asked Scott.

"Well, my parents both work at the store, but Greg is usually home, dealing with colleges and stuff," he said. "That's why I doubt the thief will go after one of our cars, since there's always someone home."

Phoebe shrugged. "All right, I guess you do have a point. I should get home, anyway. Mom probably has dinner ready."

"Me too," said Erica and Scott.

"Alright, I'll see you guys tomorrow," said Adrian. They all went back home, ate dinner, took showers and went to bed.

# Chapter VII

It wasn't until the next morning that something unexpected happened.

Phoebe climbed out of bed and stretched her arms. She changed out of her pajamas and walked downstairs to eat breakfast. To her surprise, Officer McKinley was sitting at the dining room table, talking with her parents.

"Phoebe, this is Officer McKinley," her dad said. "He would like to ask you some questions."

"Uhh..yes, we've met before," said Phoebe. "Is this about the stalker?"

"Not exactly," McKinley said. "Here, take a seat." He gestured to an empty chair at the table.

Confused, Phoebe sat down and asked, "What's this all about?"

"Your principal, Principal Peterson, had his car stolen last night," McKinley said. "We scraped through video footage from cameras around his house at that time, and we found something rather unexpected."

"No footage?" asked Phoebe.

"Well, that's what we expected," said McKinley, "But it appears as though you may have slipped up this time."

"Me?" Phoebe said, even more confused. "What did I do?"

McKinley slid a laptop over to Phoebe and plugged in a thumb drive. He opened a video on the thumb drive and said, "This was taken from a security camera that's facing the road near your principal's house."

The video was timestamped at 1:30am last night and was basically just a video of the road near Principal Peterson's garage.

"I'm really not following," said Phoebe, watching the footage. "It's just...wait." A figure had emerged into frame of the camera. Phoebe couldn't tell who it was at first, but as the figure came closer to the camera, the face became clearer. The camera quality wasn't the best and it was in black and white, but Phoebe could easily recognize the person in the video.

Phoebe gasped. "That's...not possible," she said. She went back to the figure and zoomed in, but there was no denying it. The person in the footage was her!

McKinley nodded. "I'm sure you understand my suspicions now."

"Phoebe, what were you doing there so late at night?" Phoebe's mom asked. "You realize how suspicious this looks."

"Mom, I wasn't there," Phoebe protested. "I never even got out of bed last night."

"The footage says different," said McKinley. "And you know what kind of implications this footage gives, right?"

"What? No! You don't think I stole those cars, do you?" Phoebe asked.

"I don't know," said McKinley. 'I don't like to accuse people without hard evidence, but this video shows that you were the only one there at the time of the theft."

"I told you! I wasn't there!" Phoebe protested. "Unless I sleepwalk, I didn't leave my room at all last night."

"Phoebe, stop," Phoebe's dad broke in. "We are looking at evidence that clearly shows you at your principal's garage at 1:30 in the morning. Just tell us why you were there and this whole matter of stealing cars can be cleared."

Phoebe shook her head. "I'm telling you. I don't know where that footage came from, but I promise you that I didn't leave the house."

McKinley sighed. "Look, if you won't admit that you were there and why you were there, I'm afraid I have to arrest you for suspicions of car theft."

"Hang on, I'm sure that's not necessary Officer," Phoebe's dad said. "I'm sure there's a reasonable explanation for all this."

"Well, Phoebe, I'm waiting," McKinley said. "You've got two choices here."

"For the last time, I wasn't there!" Phoebe said. "The footage was probably doctored. Isn't the car thief also a hacker? Maybe he planted this footage of me."

McKinley shook his head. "Sorry Phoebe, but this footage was part of a larger video. It would be nearly impossible to create a fake video like this. The video is too detailed and smooth to be a computer-created video."

"Well then, I've got nothing," Phoebe said. "But I swear that I didn't leave the house."

"Unfortunately, I can't accept that as proof, so I'm going to have to arrest you, Phoebe," McKinley said, grimly.

"For suspicion of car theft?" Phoebe said, flabbergasted. "I'm 14, I don't even have a license, much less the ability to hack into security cameras."

"Well, you yourself said it wouldn't be that hard to hack into a camera," said McKinley. "And you being 14 doesn't exactly help your case, considering that all the cars stolen were driven recklessly and the driver ran into countless things."

"This is absurd," said Phoebe. "You can't possibly believe that I'm the mastermind behind the car thefts. Me, a 14-year-old girl, the genius behind the thefts of what? 6 cars? Besides, I have an alibi for all the other times a car was stolen."

"Well, nobody said anything about you stealing all the cars. It could have just been this one," McKinley responded.

"And where would I hide this stolen car?" demanded Phoebe.

"Look, Phoebe. I don't believe that you actually stole Mr. Peterson's car. I just need to know what you were doing at his house so late at night," McKinley said, exasperated.

"We've been through this already," Phoebe answered, sighing. "I'm being framed by the real thief. I don't know how he did it, but that footage has been doctored somehow."

"Alright, then." The officer grasped Phoebe's arm and said "Phoebe Mason, I am placing you under arrest for car theft. You have the right to remain-"

"Seriously? Car theft?" Phoebe said. "You're arresting me for car theft? Can you even legally do this?"

"Well, I do have an arrest warrant and probable cause, so yes," McKinley said.

"Probable cause? What probable cause?" Phoebe asked.

"Really officer, this isn't necessary," said Phoebe's mom. "I'm sure Phoebe had no part in any car theft."

"I'm sorry ma'am, I really am, but since Phoebe was caught at the crime scene a few minutes before the robbery and she won't tell us what she was doing there, it's my job to arrest her," McKinley said.

"I wasn't there," Phoebe said through gritted teeth.

"Alright, let's go," said McKinley, walking to his car outside. Phoebe followed him, shaking her head.

"Now what happens?" Phoebe asked, after she was sitting in the back of the police car. "Am I seriously getting arrested right now?"

McKinley nodded. "Yes, you are. Of course, if you just explain what you were-"

"Okay, enough." Phoebe shut the car door and McKinley started the car. "So, where are we going?"

"I'm going to take you to a holding cell in the police station," McKinley answered.

"I'm going to *jail*?" Phoebe asked, incredulously. "Do I at least get a lawyer?"

"Well, naturally you get a lawyer," McKinley replied. "But it's really not necessary. You're not exactly going to jail, just to a holding cell. And while you technically are under arrest, you aren't going on trial for car theft anytime soon. So, I'd hold off with the lawyers for now."

Phoebe shook her head again. "What about school and all my science project?"

"Well, once you're released, everything will go back to normal. School included." McKinley said. "And I'll make sure to let your friends know where you are."

"Thanks," Phoebe said sarcastically. She leaned back in her seat, asking herself what was happening and trying to mentally sort through all the chaos. McKinley turned a corner and stopped at the police station. He opened Phoebe's door and Phoebe climbed out of the car. McKinley led Phoebe into the police and brought her into the holding cell near his office.

"You're actually making me stay here?" Phoebe asked. "I already told you; I didn't do anything!"

"So you've told me," McKinley said, closing and locking the cell door. "But unless you can prove otherwise, I can't release you."

"How am I supposed to prove that I was lying in bed at 1:30am if I'm locked in a jail cell?" Phoebe asked disdainfully.

"Well, you're free to talk to whoever you want, as long as they come visit you," said McKinley. "But I think it'd be easier if you just told me what you were doing at the crime scene instead of trying to prove that you weren't, when you clearly were."

"Great," said Phoebe. She said down on the bench in the cell and stretched her arms. "At least I get extra sleep, but I'm missing my classes."

"Don't worry; I'm sure your teacher will let you make the work up," said McKinley, leaving the room.

The hours didn't exactly speed by for Phoebe. Her parents were working, and Scott, Adrian, and Erica were still in school, so she was alone, except for the occasional officer popping his head in.

After the third time an officer checked on her, she said "What's the point of you constantly checking on me? I'm not going to escape or anything."

"Well, it's just protocol," the officer replied. "Plus, I don't want to be held responsible if you do escape."

After about 3 hours in, Phoebe was already incredibly bored. Officer McKinley had taken her cell phone, so she couldn't talk to anyone, and there wasn't a whole lot in the cell. When an officer popped his head in the 4$^{th}$ time, Phoebe asked him for some paper and a pencil. The officer gave her some and she started solving trig problems. This made the time go faster, so she started drawing schematics for her science experiment.

Officer McKinley brought her some food for lunch, and as Phoebe expected, it was about as good as school lunch. Since she ate school lunch pretty much every day, she was used to it. Finally, 3pm rolled around and school ended.

As Phoebe expected, Scott, Erica, and Adrian all came to visit her and figure out what was going on.

"What happened?" Scott asked. "Officer McKinley didn't really give us a lot of details."

"I really have no idea," said Phoebe. "All I know is that there's some security footage of me at Principal Peterson's garage at 1:30 in the morning, when his car was stolen. Now I'm arrested for potential car theft."

"What were you doing out at 1:30?" Adrian asked.

"Seriously?" Phoebe asked. "I wasn't out at all. I was lying in my bed, fast asleep at 1:30."

"That doesn't make sense," said Erica. "Officer McKinley showed us the footage and it was clearly you in the video."

"I know, I know," said Phoebe, exasperated. "That's why I'm in here, apparently. I think the real thief is trying to frame me."

"How exactly, though?" Scott asked. "I can't imagine how much video editing it would take to create a fake video of someone."

"It's pretty much impossible," said Phoebe. "But so is me being outside at 1 in the morning."

"So, in the words of Sherlock Holmes, 'Once you eliminate the impossible, whatever remains, no matter how improbable, must be the truth'", Adrian said.

"Okay, that's great," said Phoebe. "The only problem is, there's nothing left. The only two options are that the video is fake, or that I was actually there. And, we've already established that neither of those are possible."

"Well, not necessarily," said Scott. Everyone turned to him. "What do you mean?" asked Erica.

"Well, maybe the video isn't fake," Scott said.

"Not following you..." said Adrian.

"Let me finish. The video of Phoebe might not be fake, but the time might be," Scott said. "I took a video editing course about a year ago, and I used to insert parts of videos into other videos. The cuts weren't usually that smooth, but if someone who knew what they were doing edited that video, it probably wouldn't be that hard to make it look believable, especially on such low-quality footage."

"So, what exactly are you saying?" Phoebe asked. "You think that someone took old footage that was taken at a different time and edited into the footage from the security camera?"

"That's exactly what I'm saying," said Scott. "It's the only plausible explanation."

"What about the watermark?" asked Erica. "It clearly shows the time."

"That can easily be faked as well," said Scott. "Pretty sure you just have to change the date and time on your computer."

"Okay, so assuming all this is correct," said Phoebe, "How are we supposed to prove this?"

"We just need to find the original footage," said Scott. "I'll ask Officer McKinley what camera that footage was taken from and I'll ask the owner if I can see the past footage."

"What about me?" asked Phoebe. "Am I just supposed to sit here?"

"Pretty much," said Erica. "I brought you your Trig textbook, though. I figured you would want some entertainment."

"Oh, you're a lifesaver, Erica," Phoebe said. "I was dying of boredom in here."

Erica laughed. "You're the only person I know that could study Trig while in jail," she said.

"Is there anything else you need?" asked Scott.

"Well, my Chemistry textbook would be helpful," Phoebe said. "I'd like to get caught up on what I missed. And my Biology textbook. AP History would be great too."

"How about we just bring you all your textbooks," asked Adrian.

"That works," said Phoebe.

"Cool, we'll see you in a bit," said Scott. "I'll let you know what happens."

# Chapter VIII

They all left the building, leaving Phoebe to explore her Trig textbook. They met Officer McKinley in the hall, and Scott asked him what camera the footage came from.

"Well, I think the camera belonged to Mr. Peterson. I believe it was on his garage." McKinley answered.

"Thanks!" Scott said. He, Erica, and Adrian left the police station and headed off to Mr. Peterson's house, Scott and Adrian on their bikes and Erica on her Segway. When they got the house, Erica knocked on the door, and the principal opened the door.

"Oh, good afternoon, Erica. Scott. Adrian," the principal said, "How can I help you?"

"Hi Principal Peterson," Erica answered. "We were hoping that you could do us a favor."

"Well, that depends what the favor is, but I'll be happy to help if I can," the principal said, gesturing for them to come inside. They all stepped inside and Scott said "So, I assume that you heard about Phoebe?"

"Of course. I can't understand what on Earth she could have been doing around my driveway so late at night," the principal answered.

"Well, that's the thing," Erica broke in. "We don't believe she was. We think she's being framed."

"Framed? Now how would someone go about doing that?" Peterson asked. "There's very clear footage of her on camera."

"Well, it's hard to explain," said Scott. "But we were hoping you could help us prove that she was framed."

"What did you have in mind?" asked Peterson.

"We were hoping that you would let us see your previous footage from the camera that recorded Phoebe," Adrian said.

"I don't see why not," Peterson said. "It's all stored on my computer in my office."

The principal walked over to his office and the group followed him. He opened a folder on his computer and a list of videos popped up.

"I've only had this camera for a month, but it's been recording every day. It saves each day as a new video file. What day did you want to see?"

Adrian scratched his head and looked at Scott and Erica. "Well, we're not sure exactly. We think that the video with Phoebe in it was taken at a different time then the watermark showed, and we're hoping that we can find that footage from this camera to prove that the video was edited."

"That will be quite a challenge," Peterson said. "There's over 700 hours of video footage stored here, and I don't know where you'd even begin."

"Well, let's start by looking at the video taken last night," said Scott. "Maybe we can spot something that will help us figure out the actual time."

"Of course." Peterson opened a video in the folder and skipped ahead a few hours. He played the video of Phoebe near his house, and they all watched closely.

"I'm not seeing anything," said Adrian. "It looks about right to me."

"Well, the light from the video is from my garage lights," Peterson said. "And those only turn on at night, so the video was definitely taken at night."

"Okay, so that narrows it down to about 350 hours of video to watch," said Erica.

"Not really," said Adrian. "Phoebe wouldn't be outside past 10pm, and it doesn't get dark until 8pm in Summer, so that's only 2 hours per day."

"That's still 60 hours," said Erica "Nobody has time to sit and watch 60 hours of security camera footage."

"Well, let's split it up then," said Scott. "Mr. Peterson, can you copy this folder onto this flash drive?" Adrian pulled a 32gb flash drive out of his backpack.

"Sure, just plug it into the computer." Scott connected the flash drive into the computer and the principal copied all the video files onto the drive.

"Perfect," said Scott. "We can each take 20 hours of video. If you put it at 2x speed, we can shorten it to 10 hours, which will probably be split up between multiple days." He pulled the flash drive out of the computer and zipped up his backpack. "Thanks for your help, Principal Peterson. We'll see you at school on Monday."

"Of course," replied the principal. "I certainly hope that Phoebe was not the one who stole my car, although I will admit that the evidence seems stacked against her."

Adrian, Erica, and Scott left the principal's house and headed outside. "Let's all go to my house where we can divvy up the footage," Adrian suggested.

"We're seriously watching 60 hours of Mr. Peterson's garage?" asked Erica. "That's about as exciting as watching paint dry."

"Well, 60 hours combined; only 20 hours for each of us," Scott said. "Look, this is the only way to prove that Phoebe is being framed."

"Fine," muttered Erica. "But she owes me for this. I still have homework, you know."

"Maybe it would be easier to just find software that can recognize faces in videos," Adrian suggested. "That would be way faster than watching all that footage."

"I have programs that can do that," said Scott, "But the quality from the camera is too low for the software to work."

"Okay, you win," said Erica. "But I'm putting this video at 5x speed. I'm not watching 20 hours of a garage."

"Whatever. Just don't miss the section of footage," said Scott. He hopped on his bike and started pedaling away.

"Wait, this is dumb!" Adrian yelled to Scott. Scott hit his brakes and backtracked back to Adrian and Erica. "What do you mean?" he asked.

"Doesn't Phoebe have a photographic memory?" asked Adrian. "I'm sure she'd remember when she was at Principal Peterson's house."

Scott shrugged. "Okay, we can ask her, but if she doesn't remember, you're not getting out of watching these videos."

"Okay, fine by me," said Adrian. "Let's go to the police station, then." Adrian hopped on his bike and Erica on her Segway and they left for the police station. When they got there, they asked the receptionist if they could see Phoebe, but the receptionist said, "Sorry honey, not right now. She's in the interrogation room, but y'all are welcome to wait."

"The interrogation room?" Scott asked. "What is this, a murder trial?"

The receptionist shrugged. "Look honey, I don't know what to tell ya. I'm just the receptionist; they don't tell me nothin'. Feel free to take a seat on that bench over there and wait for it to end." She gestured towards a leather bench near the door and went back to looking at her computer.

Scott shook his head in disbelief. "Seriously? What do they want from Phoebe? It's not like she knows anything about any car thefts."

"Well, they don't know that," said Erica. "They're just doing their job."

"It doesn't take a genius to figure out that a 14-year old is not stealing cars," Scott said, annoyed.

"Look at is this way," said Adrian. "In their eyes, Phoebe was at the scene of the crime when the car was stolen. I doubt that they think that she was the one who stole the car, but they probably think that she might know something."

"Yeah, but she wasn't there!" exclaimed Scott.

"They don't know that," said Adrian. "They saw her on camera, and they have no reason to believe otherwise."

"Well, they should know that!" Scott said. "It's-"

"Scott, calm down," said Adrian. "The police are just trying to find the stolen cars and if they think that Phoebe had something to do with it, they are going to question her. Besides, we're not that far from being able to prove her innocence. We just have to watch the videos."

Scott took a deep breath. "Okay, you're right. The police are just doing their job."

Meanwhile, Phoebe was sitting in the interrogation room, across from Officer McKinley who was holding a notepad and a clipboard.

"Officer," asked Phoebe. "Was the use of handcuffs really necessary?" McKinley had placed Phoebe in a pair of handcuffs and she found them to be extremely uncomfortable and stiff.

"It's just a safety measure," McKinley said. "Relax."

"Safety measure?" asked Phoebe scornfully. "You think I'm going to jump out and attack you?"

"No, it's just- Look, Phoebe, why won't you just cooperate with us?" McKinley asked. "We just want to know what you were doing out so late and so near to the crime scene."

Phoebe rolled her eyes. "Stop asking me that. I've already told you, I wasn't even there. Someone planted that footage in order to frame me. Now can I go home?"

"Sorry Phoebe, I'm afraid that I can't allow you to go home unless you tell me what you were doing or if you can provide sufficient evidence that proves that the footage was fake."

"Isn't that your job?" asked Phoebe. "You're supposed to be looking for evidence, not me."

"No, my job is to find out who the car thief is, and right now, you're a suspect," McKinley answered.

"Well, go do your job and figure out who the real thief is, instead of wasting your time, questioning me!" Phoebe exclaimed.

McKinley sighed "Okay, we're getting nowhere. Let's try from a different angle. Where were you at 1am yesterday night?"

"In bed. Sleeping."

"Okay, and can you verify that?" McKinley asked.

"How am I supposed to verify that I was in bed?" Phoebe asked. "This interrogation is ridiculous; I'm not answering any more of your questions."

"Look, just work with me here, Phoebe," said McKinley. "I'm just trying to catch the car thief and you're making my job that much more difficult."

Phoebe ignored him and leaned back in her chair. McKinley sighed again. "Fine, this interview is over," he said. He uncuffed Phoebe's hands walked her out of the room, back into the cell.

As he was leaving his officer, he passed Adrian, Scott, and Erica sitting on the bench.

"Officer McKinley, is the interrogation done?" Adrian asked.

McKinley nodded. "Feel free to talk to her now. She won't tell me anything."

"Well, that's because you're asking her about something she has no idea about," Erica said. "That footage was edited and we're trying to find proof right now."

McKinley wiped his brow and said "This car thief has me running ragged. We've never had a string of robberies like this before in this town. So tell Phoebe that I'm sorry if I'm being a little harsh, but I'm just trying to find the thief, and that footage is the best lead we have."

"We understand, but as we've been trying to say, the footage is fake," said Scott. "Trust me, everybody in this town wants this thief to be caught, but you're barking up the wrong tree."

McKinley raised his hat. "Well, I sure hope you're right. Phoebe's a smart girl, and I hope she hasn't tangled with the wrong crowd. But if

I don't investigate her at all, the town will have my job." He wiped his brow again and left the police station, leaving the group alone.

The group headed over to Phoebe's cell where they found her solving Trig problems. The paper that the officer had given her was covered in problems and the pencil was almost down to a stub.

"Phoebe, we have a question to ask you," said Scott.

"Great, more questions," Phoebe said irritably. "I've already been asked so many questions today, I don't need more."

"Don't worry, it's to help prove your innocence," said Scott. "We just need to know if you remember all the times that you've been to Principal Peterson's house, or down his street. You have a photographic memory after all."

"I don't know," said Phoebe. "Maybe. I can't really think about anything right now. I've been sitting here for 8 hours with nothing but Trig and Biology to keep me company. And that stupid officer keeps asking me questions about things I have no idea about."

"You need something that can keep your mind occupied," said Adrian. "I'll get you your other textbooks next time we come by."

"Thanks," said Phoebe. "And I can't remember all the times that I've walked past Principal Peterson's house. Normally I would, but my brain is all foggy right now."

"It's fine," said Scott. "But we got all the footage from the camera from Principal Peterson's camera, and we're going to try and find the duplicate footage."

"You guys are great," said Phoebe. "And tell that Officer McKinley that I'd like to give him a piece of my mind."

"He's not the villain here," said Erica. "He's just trying to find the car thief and he thinks you're a suspect. The real villain here is the person who framed you and is stealing the cars."

"He still won't listen to reason," said Phoebe. "And he hasn't really done a whole lot to find the thief."

"Well, he's trying," said Scott. "We'll go through the footage and see what we can find. One of us will drop off your textbooks in a bit."

Erica, Scott, and Adrian left the police station and Scott said "Let's go to my house instead of Adrian's. It's closer, and I have a faster computer." Erica and Adrian agreed and they took off for Scott's house. It took them a while, since the police station was a good 4 miles from Scott's home, and when they got there, Scott knocked on the door.

# Chapter IX

Greg opened the door with a distressed look on his face and said "Scott, there you are! You're never going to believe this, but my car has been stolen now!"

"Wait, what?" Scott asked. "Weren't you home all day?"

"I left for about 20 minutes to walk to the post office. I needed mail a letter and when I got back, my car was gone from the garage," Greg said, practically panicking.

"How long ago was this?" asked Adrian. "Did you call the police?"

"It was only about 10 minutes ago. "I tried to call the police station, but all the phones are down."

"10 minutes, okay, we still have time!" Scott exclaimed. He tossed his bag into the house and sprinted to the home computer. Adrian and Erica followed him, confused, leaving Greg at the front door.

"Scott, fill us in! What do we still have time for?" asked Erica.

"Last night, I installed a backup program that automatically uploaded the footage from the garage camera into a cloud drive. I wanted to protect our cars in case the thief came after them. I just hope that the hacker hasn't noticed the backup program yet and deleted the footage."

Scott opened up a cloud drive on the computer and sighed with relief when he saw that the footage was still there. He grabbed a flash drive off the desk next to him and downloaded the files to the drive. No more than 30 seconds after he had finished, the file disappeared and the program with the cloud drive crashed.

Scott instantly yanked the flash drive out of the computer and said "Okay, I think I got the footage. The hacker can't delete it if I have it stored on a flash drive."

"Okay, but how do we watch that video?" asked Adrian. "The minute we plug it into a computer, the hacker deletes it."

"I have a laptop that's not connected to the internet," said Scott. "He can't get to it if it's completely offline."

Scott ran to his room, and the rest of the group followed him. He dug around in a drawer filled with random stuff, and pulled out a giant, clunky laptop. He powered on the laptop, which took a good 5 minutes. When the computer finally booted up, Scott plugged the flash drive into the USB port and played the video.

He skipped to the time where the car was being stolen, and they all watched intently as a person dressed in jeans, a t-shirt, and a baseball cap came into view. None of them could see his face, so they watched as he climbed into the car and shut the door. The couldn't see what the man was doing in the car, but after about a minute, the car started up and the man started backing the car out of the garage.

He had to turn his head to look out the window, however, and when he did, the camera caught a clear image of his head through the rear window. Scott paused the video and zoomed in.

"Anybody recognize him?" asked Scott.

"No, but that hat...it looks really familiar," said Erica. "I just don't know where I've seen it."

"He's a complete stranger to me," said Adrian.

"Let's get this footage to the police-" Scott started saying, when Erica interrupted him. "Ah-ha! I remember where I've seen this hat. It's the same hat that the guy who attacked me and Phoebe a few days ago was wearing."

"Coincidence? I think not," said Scott. "We need to get this to Officer McKinley ASAP."

"Then let's go!" said Erica. Scott pulled the flash drive out of the laptop and they all ran downstairs to their bikes/Segways and headed off to the police station, leaving Greg wondering what was going on.

They had traveled for about a mile, when Erica pointed to something behind them. It was a black SUV moving very slowly, and it seemed to be tailing them. Erica pulled her Segway closer to Scott and Adrian and said "Guys, we have a problem."

She gestured to the car traveling behind them and they both looked back. "It has to be the thief," said Adrian. "He must be trying to get the flash drive from us."

"Well, what do we do?" asked Erica. "We're still a couple miles away from the police station, and there's no way we can outrun them."

"Just keep biking normally," said Scott. "There's an alley that we can turn down. It's coming up in a few blocks, and they won't able follow us there."

The never made it to the alley though. About a quarter of a mile later, the man sped up and pulled up next to them. He leaned his head out the window and asked, "Hey, do you know where the closest gas station is here?"

Nervously, Scott said "Uhh, I think it's a few miles that way," he said, pointing ahead of him.

"Yeah, that's the closest one there is," Erica and Adrian agreed.

"Thanks, appreciate it!" said the man. He leaned back into the car, but instead of going in the direction that Scott had pointed, he turned the wheel to the left and rammed the side of the car into Scott's bike. Scott's wheel bent and he went flying off his bike, into Adrian and Erica, shoving them off their vehicles and onto the grass next to the road.

Dazed, they tried to get to their feet and run, but the man sprayed a can of knockout gas onto them, causing their throats to burn and for them to get dizzy. They tried to fight the effects of the gas, but eventually they all passed out.

# Chapter X

When Scott awoke, he found himself in a large, empty room. Still dizzy, he blinked a few times and tried to figure out where he was, but the room was dark, and he could barely see anything.

"Scott. Scott!" Erica whispered loudly. "Are you awake?"

"Erica?" Scott turned his head in the direction of the voice. "Where are you?" Scott tried to rub his eyes, but realized that he was tied to a chair.

"Over here," Erica whispered from a few feet away. "Are you okay?"

"I think so," Scott whispered back. He could feel a few cuts and bruises, but nothing hurt too badly. "Where's Adrian?"

"I think he's a few feet away from me," whispered Erica. "He hasn't woken up yet, though."

"Where are we?" asked Scott.

"I can't tell. It's too-" Erica was interrupted by the footsteps of a person approaching them. The lights turned on and Scott went blind for a few seconds. He blinked a few times and looked in the direction of the footsteps. There was a man walking towards them, holding something in his hand. He was wearing a black mask that covered everything except his eyes, but he was wearing the distinctive baseball cap that Erica recognized as the cap that the person in the video and the person who had attacker her and Phoebe had been wearing.

"Ah, good, you're finally awake," he said. "Now, I believe you have something that I want, don't you?"

Scott shook his head. "I don't know what you're talking about."

"Do not play dumb with us, kid," a woman's voice said from behind them. Scott and Erica turned their heads and saw a woman also wearing a mask walking towards them. "We both know what we're looking for."

Scott gave a puzzled look and said "Sorry, I think you have the wrong person. I have no idea what you are talking about."

"The flash drive, you idiot!" The man brandished the thing he was holding in his hand. "We can either do this the easy way or the hard way. We already searched your backpack, but there was no flash drive, so you're hiding it somewhere. Where is it?"

Mentally, Scott smiled. He had made sure to remove the flash drive from his backpack and hide it as soon as they spotted the car. To the man he said, "No idea what you're talking about."

The man growled and turned to Erica. "How about you? You want to start talking, or are we going to have to do this the hard way?"

Erica gave the man a nasty look. "Even if I knew what you were talking about, I wouldn't tell you."

"You sure?" the man asked. "You of all people know what I can do." He gestured to the cast on Erica's leg.

Erica ignored him and looked over at Adrian, who was still unconscious. "What did you do to him?" she asked the man.

"Oh, nothing," the woman said. "He just seems to have a worse reaction to the gas then you two. I'm sure he'll wake up eventually. In the meantime, how about we jog your memory just a bit?"

Scott and Erica looked at the man. "Still have no idea what you're talking about," said Scott.

"Very well then," the man said. He walked closer to Scott and jabbed the item he was holding into Scott's side and pressed a button on it.

MEANWHILE, PHOEBE WAS sitting in her cell, reading her biology textbook, when she heard something coming from Officer McKinley's officer. She put down the book and listened to it. The sound was muffled by the door, but it sounded like an alarm.

She couldn't figure out what it was, until she realized what the sound was. It was coming from her phone that McKinley had taken. There was an app installed on her phone that was connected to a device that the group had bought years ago. When activated, the device sent an alarm to every phone that was paired with it, as long as the phone was on. She had totally forgotten about that app, since they basically never used those devices, but now that she heard it, she immediately realized that one of them must be in trouble.

One problem. She was locked in a cell, and Officer McKinley had gone out for coffee. She had to get the attention of someone in the police station, but how. She settled on the most efficient method: yelling. She started calling for someone's attention, and thankfully, it didn't take long for an officer to hear her.

"Pipe down, pipe down," the officer said. He looked around the room. "What is that sound?" he asked.

Phoebe pointed to the office and explained what she had deduced. The officer listened, and then burst out laughing. "Now, that's just impressive," he said, laughing.

"What?" Phoebe asked, confused. "I'm being serious, I swear. My friends could be in trouble."

"This has to be the most elaborate scheme someone your age has ever cooked up." The officer said. "Now, let me just turn that alarm off and you can relax."

He walked over to the office, and Phoebe watched helplessly. "No, stop," she begged. "If you turn off the alarm, we'll have no way of tracking them."

Just as the officer was about to turn the phone off, Officer McKinley walked into the office. "What is going on here?" he asked the officer. The officer started to explain, but Phoebe interrupted him and said, "My friends are in trouble! That's what the alarm on my phone is for. We have to go find them."

McKinley picked the phone off the desk. "You can leave now," he said to the other officer. "I'll handle this."

The officer scratched his forehead, but said "Alright Chief, if you say so," and left the room. McKinley looked at Phoebe. "Why do you say that your friends are in trouble?"

Phoebe explained the point of the app and said "We agreed only to use it in emergencies. It tracks the location of the devices, and sends and alarm to all the phones that are connected."

McKinley grabbed his belt of keys and unlocked Phoebe's cell. "Alright, let's go," he said. "But this better not be a hoax."

"It's not, I promise," said Phoebe. She followed McKinley to his car and they burned rubber.

"What's the location?" asked McKinley. Phoebe looked at her phone. "It says that the location is approximate, since wherever they are has poor signal." She showed her phone to McKinley, who punched the location into the car's GPS system.

AS SOON AS THE MAN pushed the button on the device, an electrical shock shot through Scott's entire body. It was more painful than anything he had ever felt, but he gritted his teeth and closed his eyes, trying to force the pain away.

The man let go of the button and Scott took a couple of deep breaths. "Jog your memory at all?" the man asked. Scott shook his head and said "I don't know what you mean."

The woman walked over to Erica, and took the shocker from the man. "You're quite resistant," she said to Scott. Perhaps this one will be a little less so."

She put the shocker to Erica's side, and Erica pulled against the ropes. The woman pushed the button and Erica screamed in pain. It seemed as though the woman had turned the device up and Erica's screams hurt Scott almost as much as the shocks had.

"Okay, okay, stop!" he yelled. "I'll tell you where the flash drive is." The woman let go of the button. "Well, how about that," she said. "Looks like he did know what we were talking about after all."

She walked away from Erica, who was breathing heavily and said "So, where is it?"

"It's right—"

Suddenly, there was a loud crash and both the man and the woman slumped to the ground. Scott looked up, and saw Adrian holding a smashed chair.

"What? I thought you were unconscious," said Scott. "How did you get out?"

Adrian knelt down and started untying Scott's ropes. "Having a younger sister who won't stop annoying you really helps you practice faking unconsciousness," he said. "Also, I used to be a magician for little kids, so I learned a little bit about escapology."

He finished untying Scott's ropes, and they moved over to Erica and started untying her ropes. "Are you okay?" Scott asked her.

"Should be," said Erica. "Just a little weak." Just as Scott untied the last knot, there was a stir from behind them, and Scott saw the man and woman getting up. Scott hurriedly yanked the rope off, and pulled Erica up.

"We've gotta get out of here," said Scott. It was too late, though. The man and woman were both brandishing knives and heading right towards them. In an effort to slow them down, Scott kicked a table in their direction and hit the man in the shin. Jumping off of a chair, Adrian took the man down in a flying tackle, knocking the knife out of his hand.

The man grunted and hit Adrian in the chest with a piece of wood that was lying nearby. Scott came to his rescue and kicked the man in the chest, while Erica took down the woman. Even with her cast, Erica was able to knock the woman off her feet with a few quick punches and kicks.

They had the upper hand until the man managed to shove Adrian and Scott off and hurl a chair at them. The chair hit Scott in the knee, and he went down. The man rushed over to help the woman with Erica, but Adrian blocked his way. Unfortunately, Adrian wasn't much of a fighter, and the man easily took him down.

The man pulled Erica off of the woman, despite Erica's well-placed punches and kicks, and shoved her into a pile of chairs. The woman stood up, and rubbed her side where Erica had kicked her.

"That was well done," the man said, picking up his knife. "Too bad we still have the upper hand." He clutched his knife, and walked over to where the group was sitting. He grabbed Adrian by his arm and yanked him up, holding the knife a few inches from his throat.

"Now then, one of you is going to tell me where you've hidden the flash drive, or this lovely young man will get his throat slit."

Scott raised his hands in defeat. "Put the knife down, and I'll tell you where the drive is," he said.

"Nice try, but you give me the drive first, and then I'll put the knife down," the man said, pulling the knife even closer.

"Alright then," said Scott. He reached down into his shoe and pulled out the drive. He stood up slowly and passed the flash drive over to the man. The man dropped his knife and let go of Adrian's arm. "Perfect," he said. "Now-

The door to the building suddenly swung open and Officer McKinley stood there with his gun drawn. "Police, freeze," he yelled. "Put your weapons on the ground and your hands up."

"Why you little- "The man lunged at Scott with his knife, but McKinley fired his gun and shot the man in the arm. The man shouted

in pain and fell to the ground, clutching his arm. The woman dropped her knife and put her hands in the air. Erica got up from the floor and ripped the woman's mask off.

"Wait a minute, I know who you are," she said. "You're that woman who answered the door when we went to talk to Mr. McGinnis. What were you doing there?"

"Getting information about what cars to steal, of course," the woman growled. "The old man has been living here for over 70 years. With a little bit of persuasion, it wasn't hard to get the information about the cameras and the times when people left their house."

"Great," said McKinley. "Another thing they can add to your rap sheet." He pulled the woman and the man up and handcuffed them. "Let's go," he said, pulling them to the police car.

"Officer, wait," Scott said. "Let me see their fingerprints." McKinley shrugged and turned the thieves around so Scott could look at their fingerprints. Scott examined them and then said. "There's another person whose helping them."

"Ridiculous," said the man. "It's just us."

"Why do you say that, Scott?" McKinley asked. Scott looked around the room and spotted his backpack. He grabbed it and dug through it until he found the bag with the tape in it. He showed it to McKinley and said "This fingerprint doesn't match either of them."

"Hmm, you're right," said McKinley. "Where did you get this?"

Scott explained how he had taken it off the quarter he had found in Adrian's garden. "Sounds like a long shot," said McKinley, "But you might be right." He yanked on the thieves' arms. "Who's your partner, huh?"

"I know who it is," Erica said suddenly, standing up. "It's that boy who was trying to take a photo of me in the woods. I didn't notice this before, but I'm pretty sure I saw him at McGinnis' door when we knocked."

"Don't know any boys," muttered the man. "The girl is crazy."

"I'll bet we'll find him where we find the cars," said a voice behind McKinley.

"Phoebe!" Erica exclaimed. "I take it you got the emergency alert."

"Yes, although it would have been easier if I hadn't been locked in a jail cell." Phoebe looked at McKinley.

"Yeah, about that," said Scott. "We need to find their computer setup. It's where all the hacking gets done."

"Well, we can do all that later," said McKinley. "Let's get these dirtbags down to the police station first, and then we can question them."

McKinley radioed for another police car and had that officer take the thieves to the police station. Scott, Erica, Phoebe, and Adrian climbed into McKinley's car and McKinley drove them to the police station.

"I guess I owe you an apology, Phoebe," McKinley said. "Sorry for arresting you."

"It's fine," said Phoebe. "You were just doing your job. I'm just glad that we caught the real criminals."

"Well, we caught the criminals, but we still don't have the cars," said Adrian. "And they're not going to tell us unless we give them something, so we have to find them ourselves."

"Oh, that's easy," said Scott. "I've been meaning to tell you this, but my parents put a tracker on Greg's car. He never knew this, but since I helped put it on, I know how to access the location."

"And you're just telling us now?" asked Erica.

"Well, I remembered it when we were biking to the police station," said Scott. "I was going to suggest that we track it, and then Officer McKinley and a bunch of other officers could have a stakeout and catch the criminal when he went to check on the cars. I never exactly got that chance, though."

"So, how do we track it?" McKinley asked.

"Simple. We just send a text to this number, and it will spit back the exact coordinates of where it is." Scott sent a text to the number and it gave him the coordinates for the latitude and longitude of the car. Scott looked it up on Google Maps and McKinley said.

"That's only a few blocks from here. We should be able to get there before their third partner leaves." He stepped on the gas and zoomed to the address. They pulled up near an old warehouse with broken windows and a caving roof.

"Nice place," said McKinley. He stepped out of the car and drew his gun. "You guys stay here," he said as we walked into the building.

The teens waited anxiously for McKinley to come out, but suddenly they saw a boy dash from the building, being chased by McKinley.

"He's never going to catch him," said Adrian, who was sitting in the front seat of the car. He hopped over to the driver's seat and turned the car on.

"Adrian, what are you doing?" exclaimed Erica.

"Catching the criminal," said Adrian, stepping on the gas. He swerved around a telephone pole and a trash can, before he was finally able to cut the boy off. Scott jumped out of the car after Adrian hit the brakes, and landed a hard punch to the boy's jaw which knocked him out.

Puffing, McKinley picked the boy up by his elbows and stuck him in the backseat, next to Erica. "Recognize him?" he asked. Erica looked at the boy's face. "Well, of course. He's the dummy that tried to take a photo of me and Phoebe."

"Well, maybe he'll tell us why he wanted that photo," said Phoebe. "Well, when he wakes up at least."

McKinley looked at Adrian. "There are so many illegal things in what you just did, but I'm certainly glad you did. If you don't mind, I'd like to drive to the police station, though."

Adrian laughed and climbed out of the driver's seat. "So, are all the cars there?" he asked. McKinley nodded. "Yep. Every single one of them. I'll send a towing company out to bring the cars back to their rightful owners tomorrow."

McKinley drove back to the police station and booked all the thieves. After that, he drove Erica, Scott, and Adrian back to the place where they were held so they could pick up the stuff that the thieves had taken from them. Then he picked up their bikes, and Erica's Segway.

"Thanks for all your help with the case," McKinley said to them, once they had gotten back to the police station. "As a matter of fact, it's my honor to present with these official badges."

He handed each of them a badge that read: Honorary Detective, certified by Police Chief McKinley.

"Thanks," they all said together.

"Of course," said McKinley. "But don't get yourselves tangled in another mess like this. You guys could have been injured badly, or possibly even killed."

"Does this badge mean I won't be arrested again?" Phoebe asked.

McKinley chuckled. "As long as you don't commit any crimes, I'll make sure to give you the benefit of the doubt next time. Oh, by the way." He looked at Erica. "I asked the boy what they needed the photo for and he said that his dad wanted it to locate the video of Phoebe that they used to frame her. He felt that you two were getting too suspicious, and he wanted to get you to stop looking."

"Wait, his dad?" asked Phoebe. "They were a family?"

"Yep," said McKinley. "It was a whole family of criminals. Turns out they were going to take the cars apart and sell the parts to a chop shop a few towns over."

"So, did you find the computer that they used for hacking?" Scott asked.

"Yes, we did. We confiscated it, and all the evidence was on it. It was actually the wife who did the hacking, and the son and the dad did the driving. Also, Adrian, that quarter that was in your garden. We examined it, and it turns out it was a misprinted quarter worth over $2000," McKinley said.

"Wait, seriously?" Adrian asked. "Do I get to keep it?"

"Well, it was on your property, so I don't see any reason why not," McKinley replied, smiling

"You can sell it and use the money to repair your garden," said Erica. "We'll all help you replant your flowers."

"Wow, this is incredible! That more than covers the cost of my garden," Adrian exclaimed. "I can make my garden even better than it was before!"

"Yes, but right now, we should get you home. Your parents are waiting for you; I explained what happened." McKinley said. He gestured for them to go to the police car and McKinley dropped each of them off at their homes.

# Epilogue:

Two weeks later, Scott, Erica, Adrian, and even Phoebe were busy replanting Adrian's new garden. Complete with an automatic watering system and a metal fence to prevent damage from vehicles, Adrian was the happiest he'd ever been.

Erica's leg had healed up and she was back to playing sports, like she always did. Still captain of the soccer team, she had led her team to victory in the semi-finals and was preparing to play in the finals against the Southbrook High team.

Phoebe finished her science project with a few suggestions from Erica and like always, got first place. She proudly accepted the blue ribbon and placed it in her trophy case along with the many other accolades she'd won. The time she had spent in jail had given her time to practice for her Trig test that was coming up, and she aced it, along with getting the highest score in her class. Now the only thing left to do was prepare for the SAT.

Scott couldn't decide between a drill hand or a claw hand for his robot, so he decided to make the attachments removable, and made both a drill hand and a claw hand. In fact, the drill hand was being used to help Adrian plant seeds in his garden, and the claw and was being used to fill the holes with dirt again. Grateful to Scott for helping get his car back, Greg taught him how to drive, but only after warning him countless times to never, ever drive without someone else in the car.

All in all, it had been a fun and exciting month for each of them, but they were all looking forward to relaxing when summer break finally rolled around in a few days. Well, all of them except Phoebe, who naturally thought summer break was a waste of time and instead enrolled in a summer camp for STEM.

# The End

A novelette by Travis Cramer

# Don't miss out!

Visit the website below and you can sign up to receive emails whenever Travis Cramer publishes a new book. There's no charge and no obligation.

https://books2read.com/r/B-A-CVTIB-CTRDD

**BOOKS 2 READ**

Connecting independent readers to independent writers.

# About the Author

Travis Cramer is a 18-year-old storyteller with roots in the lively state of New Jersey. At 12, his family traded the hustle and bustle for the quieter charm of Delaware—a shift that left young Travis searching for adventure. With fewer distractions in his new surroundings, he turned to his love of fiction as an outlet for creativity. What started as a simple hobby soon transformed into a mission: to write a full-fledged story, beginning to end. From this spark of inspiration, *Misadventure and Mystery* was born—a series where imagination knows no bounds, and every page brims with excitement and intrigue.

Read more at https://books2read.com/ap/81Do3O/Travis-Cramer.